one whole and perfect day

JUDITH CLARKE

one whole and perfect day

BOYDS MILLS PRESS

AN IMPRINT OF HIGHLIGHTS

Honesdale, Pennsylvania

Originally published by Allen & Unwin, 2006

Library of Congress Cataloging-in-Publication Data

Clarke, Judith.
One whole and perfect day / Judith Clarke. —1st U.S. ed.
p. cm.
Summary: As her irritating family prepares to celebrate her
grandfather's eightieth birthday, sixteen-year-old Lily yearns for just
one whole perfect day together.
ISBN-13: 978-1-932425-95-6 (hc) • ISBN: 978-1-62091-025-2 (pb)
[1. Grandparents—Fiction. 2. Brothers and sisters—Fiction.
3. Family problems—Fiction. 4. Australia—Fiction.] I. Title.
PZ7.C55365On 2007
[Fic]—dc22
2006020126

10 9 8 7 6 5 4 3 2 1

Boyds Mills Press
815 Church Street
Honesdale, Pennsylvania 18431

one whole and perfect day

1 PROPER FAMILIES

Every day on her way home from school, Lily lingered in the quiet streets and avenues of her neighborhood gazing through the windows of the houses at the families inside. She saw kids watching TV and doing their homework and playing computer games; she saw mums and dads talking and laughing together, chopping vegetables in their kitchens, stirring pots on the stove. Proper families, Lily would think to herself, they're proper families.

Not like hers. For a start, she had no dad; he'd bolted back home to America when Lily had been no larger than a plum pip deep inside her mother. She'd never even seen her father, and when his phone messages came at Christmas and birthdays, she found she didn't know what to call him: "Dad" sounded awkward in her mouth, unnatural, like a cold hard pebble rolling behind her teeth. Her brother, Lonnie, who'd been almost six when their father had gone, experienced no such trouble. "Oh, hi, Dad," he'd murmur into the telephone, and "Oh?" and "Yeah, Dad!" and the very ease with which Lonnie said that name gave his sister a small, sharp pang, even though, on the ordinary days that made up most of her life, she hardly gave a conscious thought to her absent father.

Lily paused on the sidewalk to let a car coming home ease its way through gateposts where a clutch of bright party balloons fluttered; their round, bright perfection made her catch her breath. She watched the car door open and a man get out and two little kids race across the lawn toward him screaming, "Daddy! Daddy's home!"

Hitching her backpack more comfortably across her shoulders, Lily walked on down the street. Plenty of kids had single-parent families; she knew that, just as she knew it wasn't the absence of a father, or even the smallness of their family—only the three of them, five if you counted Nan and Pop—that made them stand out. No, thought Lily irritably, it was the sheer peculiarity of the people in it that made her family not quite right.

First there was Lonnie. But no, she wasn't going to think of Lonnie—thinking about her hopeless brother always made her angry, especially on a darkening winter afternoon when there was dinner to get on at home and tons of homework after.

She'd think of Mum instead because Mum was okay, sort of: a pale slender woman with wispy blonde hair pulled back in an untidy knot. The worst you could say of her was that she worried about Lonnie too much and worked too hard at her job—long, long hours at the day-care center, then bringing home paperwork and sometimes actual people, old people whose care-giver children were quite desperate for a little break, so Mum said. Lame ducks, Lily called them.

Mum was a softie, just like Nan. A tiny smile tweaked at Lily's lips when she thought of her nan: of her small plump figure and the soft white hair cut in a little girl's style, straight around the ears and with a thick shiny fringe down to her eyebrows; of her lavender scent and floral dresses and long droopy cardigans in pastel shades. Nan was a picture-book granny, except for one thing: she had an imaginary companion like ones little kids sometimes had, a made-up friend called Sef, who accompanied Nan most places, around the house and garden, up and down the hilly streets of Katoomba, and whom Nan addressed in a low sweet voice, offering confidences and asking Sef's opinion on anything to do with family.

When Lily was little, this had somehow seemed quite natural. "Who's Sef?" she'd asked.

"An old friend, dear."

"A girl? Is she a girl, Nan?"

"Yes, she is."

"You can't tell, from that name, can you? You can't tell if she's a boy or girl."

"No, you can't."

"And you can't see her. Is she invil, um, invilable?"

"*Invisible*, dear. Yes, Sef's invisible."

These days, at seventeen, Lily found her grandmother's companion unsettling. Could Nan—in the nicest possible way, of course—actually be a little bit daffy? Though who wouldn't be daffy if they'd been married to Pop for more than fifty years? Pop was short and loud and sturdy, red-faced even when he wasn't shouting. Pop bristled—he wore his gray hair in the kind of spiky crew cut that reminded you of cops and soldiers and the kind of people who glared at migrants in the street and told them to go back where they came from. Pop had actually been a cop once, though never a soldier because he had flat feet, and Lily thought he was a bit of a racist, too, or at least the sort of reactionary old person who thought a decent Aussie was the best kind of person in the world.

Lily quickened her step. She was very close to home now; just three more houses and she'd reach the corner of her own street, Roslyn Avenue. And always as she reached this corner,

Lily would stop dead. She'd close her eyes and count to five, slowly, before she turned into her street. She knew it was ridiculous, the kind of thing a very little kid would do, like skipping cracks or crossing the road to avoid a black cat in your path—and yet Lily couldn't stop herself; she *had* to do it, because when turning that corner she was always seized by a panic that their house would be gone, nothing left of it except a pile of smoking dust and ashes and a thin trickle of smoke rising up above the trees of Roslyn Avenue and escaping into the sky.

And this was all Pop's fault, just as he'd been the one responsible for Lonnie's leaving home last January. Pop hated their house. He said it was a dump. He said it was unsanitary and falling down, though not falling fast enough for him. "I could burn it down for you," he kept on offering. "When you're out, of course. You'd get a fortune for the land, and with the insurance you could buy yourself a really decent place. Something fit for human habitation ..."

"No *thanks!*" Lily always told him, and her mum would murmur, smiling at him, "Oh, Dad, really!"

"He'd never do it," Mum said, but Lily wasn't quite so sure. There was something unpredictable about Pop, even though he was so old. Hadn't he threatened Lonnie with an ax? Told him that if he dropped out of one more course or one more job, he'd feel the edge of it? What kind of grandfather was that, anyway? Grandfathers were supposed to be kind and understanding, sympathetic to their grandchildren's problems, weren't they? Lonnie hadn't even done anything, nothing out of the ordinary, that was; he was simply being his same old useless self, and all at once Pop had lost his block completely.

"One, two, three, four—five!" counted Lily, and she

stepped bravely round the corner into Roslyn Avenue, where she saw at once, as she always did, that the house was still standing. There it was! Porch sagging, paint peeling, the windows crowded so thickly with ivy that even at the height of summer there was hardly any light inside.

"Mummy, I want to go home!" the small daughter of a charity collector had bellowed a few days earlier when Mum asked them into the house while she went in search of her purse. "This is the Witch's Cottage!"

It *was* like the Witch's Cottage, Lily thought, and yet she loved every crack and cranny of it, every leak and stain.

"Is that stain on the ceiling of my room still there?" Lonnie had asked the last time she'd talked to him on the telephone at the Boarding House for Gentlemen where he was living now. "The one shaped like a cauliflower?"

"'Course it is."

"You know, I really miss it. When I'm lying on my bed thinking—"

And that would be most of the time, thought Lily, though she didn't say it, because calls from Lonnie were rare.

"And I look up," he continued, "and the ceiling's ... bare. It seems really funny not to see the old cauliflower."

Yes, their house was a dump, thought Lily, forcing the gate open and closing her ears to the unearthly shriek it made as it scraped across the concrete, but it was dear and familiar, too. Even if it wasn't proper, it was home, and it was theirs.

2 THE SENSIBLE ONE OF THE FAMILY

Lily was the sensible one of the family. She always had been. She could write her name and count to fifty before she started school, and even tie her own shoelaces, something her mum said Lonnie hadn't learned till he was in Grade Three. By age seven she was getting her big brother up for school in the mornings, since he never seemed to hear Mum's pleadings. These days, she cooked dinner every second night, made out the shopping list for Saturday, and remembered when the car had to be serviced and bills paid.

Yes, she was the sensible one—but there were times, like this evening, alone in the gloomy old kitchen, swinging the fridge door open to gather the ingredients for spaghetti sauce, when Lily wished she wasn't. She wished she was like the other girls in Year Ten, like Lizzie Banks or Lara Reid or even awful Tracy Gilman. She wished she could, just once, *enjoy* filling in a quiz from *Bestie* without thinking it was bullshit, or talk about clothes without suddenly remembering the funny noise the washing machine had started making and how much it might cost to get it fixed.

Like someone's *mother*, thought Lily with disgust, as she took carrots and onions and parsley from the vegetable crisper and began to chop. Like someone's *Nan*.

The carrots were old and tough, the knife slid, Lily nicked her finger and almost felt like crying. Another tiny cut—even her hands didn't look like real girls' hands, covered as they were with tiny cuts and household scratches. "What do you *do*?" Tracy Gilman had demanded the day before when the 10B girls, gathered in their special lunchtime place beneath the pepper trees, were comparing the shapes of their fingernails. "What on earth do you do to get your hands looking so gross?"

"Nothing," Lily had replied defensively, snatching her hands away, and then, more robustly, "I've got a pet piranha," because anything was better than saying that she did housework. And though she did it, lots of it, Lily wasn't all that skilled: the most tender meat grew stringy when she cooked it, her gravy had lumps, cheese sauce curdled … she wasn't a bit like Nan. Lily pictured her grandmother in the kitchen, busy at her spotlessly scrubbed table, so calm and efficient— perhaps all that housework, years and years and years of it, was responsible for poor old Nan's delusion that she had an imaginary companion. Perhaps one day, not too far away down the track, Lily herself would begin to see another person standing at the kitchen bench beside her, shadowy at first, and then becoming clearer. Lily shuddered, and the knife slipped again, narrowly missing another finger. She chucked the tough old carrot in the bin and started on the onions. Started, and then, quite suddenly, stopped, flinging the knife down on the bench. Why did everything come down to her?

She knew the answer. Because Mum was overworked, and Lonnie had moved out of home, though even when he'd lived here, in household matters her brother hadn't been much use. He was … well, Lily couldn't think of words for Lonnie, only pictures, tiny incidents that somehow said it all: Lonnie helping her with the shopping one dark wet day last year, snatching the three-liter jug of orange juice from the shopping cart and holding up another brand. "*This* one!"

"What?"

"P and N!" He'd pointed to the label.

"P and N. So?"

"Don't you get it? Pop and Nan. See?"

He was like a toddler. At the cheese counter he'd taken a fancy to *La vache qui rit*.

"But that's cream cheese, Lon. We don't use it. We need ordinary stuff, the sort you use in macaroni and cheese."

He'd pulled a face, toddler-style.

She'd picked up a block of supermarket cheddar. "This kind. See?"

He'd wagged his head. "Yeah, but—"

Lily had dropped the block of cheese into the cart.

"Okay, Lil, you know best, but—"

"But what?"

"Oh, nothing." He'd flicked at the heavy lock of hair that fell across his forehead. It had stayed there. He'd flicked again. And again.

"Oh, leave it!" Lily had hissed.

Outside in the street it had been raining. Mum had been home with the flu. Lon had just dropped out of his economics course. The fridge was packing up, and the person Lonnie called Dad had forgotten to phone Lily on her birthday. Not that she cared about that; he always did it, forgot and then phoned ten months later, upsetting her all over again. Once he'd even got her name wrong. He had called her Lolly. *Lolly!* It was strange how someone you didn't know could make you feel, even if only for a few brief hours, as if you didn't matter.

A wind from the Arctic had scoured their faces as they emerged from the supermarket, and on the median strip in the middle of the highway, perched dangerously between two roaring streams of traffic, Lon had grabbed her arm. "We needed something laughing," he'd said.

"What?"

"That's why I wanted it, the cream cheese. So there'd be something in the house that laughs. Even if it was only the cheese. *La vache qui rit*. 'The cow that laughs.'"

She couldn't help noticing how perfect his accent was, how he'd sounded exactly like Mme. Robert at school. So how come he'd failed his oral French exam back in Year Twelve? Lonnie was a total mystery. Trucks and cars had roared around their tiny traffic island, the rain had pelted down, and Lonnie's face had gone vague and dreamy, as if his soul had been beamed up to some distant corner of the universe and only his shell was left here for Lily and Mum to mind. When a break came in the traffic, she had to tweak at his arm. "C'mon," she'd said gently, as if he were some frail and helpless creature she'd taken for a walk. "C'mon, Lon. Let's go home."

What would Lon be having for dinner tonight? wondered Lily, dragging herself back into the present. Now that he no longer shared their life and was out there in the big wide world on his own? Cheeseburgers from the take-out? Hot chips? Pot noodles warmed in hot water in the kitchen of the boarding house she and Mum had never seen? If it even had a kitchen …

She glanced up at the clock: almost six; Mum would soon be home. What would it be like to have a dad come in the door? Lily shook her head, took up the knife, and began to chop onions again. She thought, no matter how hard she scrubbed in the shower, the smell of them stayed in her skin and hair.

3 MARIGOLD

In her small stuffy office at the day-care center, Lily's mother Marigold closed down her computer, stretched, and yawned. It hadn't been a bad day, she reflected: no one had wandered from the premises. No frail old person had sneaked through the gates and trailed down the highway, imagining it was a Saturday night in 1937 and the Roxy dance hall just around the corner. There'd been no brawls in the recreation rooms, no accusations of theft or slander or adultery. Indeed, the afternoon had been so quiet that Marigold had found time to call Lonnie's boarding house in Toongabbie.

She hadn't been spying, she told herself. She hadn't been trying to check up that he was still doing his course, still going to his lectures and tutorials, and not lying in bed in the middle of the afternoon. The idea of Lonnie lying in bed in the middle of the afternoon haunted Marigold, bringing an even more frightening vision of a middle-aged Lonnie, stubble-chinned and gray-haired, still lying there. Or an old, old Lonnie, long after she had gone—would Lily look after him then? Would she? Marigold didn't really know; Lily was a good girl—look how she helped around the house! Look how she did the shopping! And yet Lily could be a little hard sometimes. Perhaps she'd give up on Lonnie, as Pop had, and what would happen to him then?

So when Lonnie's landlady told her he was out, Marigold couldn't help but ask, "You mean, he's at the university?"

"I believe so," replied Mrs. Rasmussen in the cool, efficient tone that made her sound more like a warden than a landlady, a stout, stern person with a bunch of keys chained round her waist, the keeper of an institution.

"I believe so." It was a vague enough answer, devoid of any hard information, yet when Marigold heard it, her mother's heart had given a small leap of joy—perhaps Lonnie would be all right after all. Perhaps he was—as Marigold had been telling everyone for years—simply a slow developer, one of those people who matured late, who, in their mid- or late twenties or early thirties, or later on—eventually, anyway—found themselves and dazzled everyone. Feeling oddly hopeful, almost lighthearted, Marigold gathered up her handbag and keys and headed for the door. It was five forty-five, and with a little bit of luck she might be home in time to help Lily with the dinner. Not that it mattered if she wasn't. Lily could cope. Lily could always be relied on. Lily was the sensible one in the family.

As she walked down the hall, Marigold heard voices coming from the recreation room. A male voice, coaxing, even deferential, seemed to be pleading with someone. "Mum? Mu-um?"

Marigold glanced through the open door and saw old Mrs. Nightingale busy with a game of solitaire at the center table. Her son hovered beside her, a gray-haired, despondent-looking man, who looked as if he might well keep to his bed in the middle of the afternoon. "Mum?" he said again.

"In a moment, Phillip." The old lady's clear voice held a trace of irritation. "I want to finish this game."

"But—"

"No buts, please. You're spoiling my concentration."

Another voice, small and mousy like some tiny anxious creature from a Beatrix Potter book (Mrs. Tittlemouse perhaps, thought Marigold), squeaked abruptly, "Hello, Dr. Samson."

Marigold peered around the edge of the door and saw Sarah, Mrs. Nightingale's daughter-in-law, seated in the big blue armchair that old Captain Cuthbert always called "my chair." He'd swing a punch at anyone who touched it, and Marigold was relieved she'd heard the Captain going home this evening, shouting at his poor daughter as they passed the office, "You're no daughter of mine!"

Sarah was sorting through a lapful of shiny travel brochures. "Going on holiday?" asked Marigold.

"Oh, I hope so." Sarah's eyes grew large in her little pointed face. She lowered her voice to a whisper. "If we can find someone to look after Mum. It's a second honeymoon, see? A romantic long weekend ..."

Jokes were made about taking mothers on your first honeymoon, thought Marigold, and obviously it was the same second time around. She found it puzzling, though, because old Mrs. Nightingale was one of the day-care center's most independent clients—mobile, all faculties intact, perfectly able to spend a few days alone. "Doesn't she like being in the house by herself?"

"She loves it!"

"So?"

"She'd burn it down, Dr. Samson! Leave something boiling on the stove! Or flood it! Leave the bath taps running!"

"Do you think so? She seems so capable to me."

Sarah's eyes grew even rounder. "Oh Dr. Samson, you don't *know*."

"Don't know what?"

Sarah twitched her tiny nose. "She gets so *immersed.*"

"Immersed?"

"In her card games. Or in those books of hers—she can read all day, Dr. Samson. Isn't that strange?"

"Well—"

"On and on and on she goes. I honestly don't think she knows she's in this world."

Marigold thought of Lonnie as a little boy, curled up on the sofa reading and reading and reading. Anything he could get his hands on, except school readers, which he left strictly alone. Marigold had once found three of them—three!—in the garbage bin.

"Ticket to outer space," whispered Sarah.

"What?" Marigold was still thinking of Lonnie.

"Those books of Mum's, the way she reads. Outer space, you know." Sarah twirled a finger at her forehead.

Marigold was beginning to dislike poor Sarah, though disliking clients' children was surely unprofessional. "I think it's perfectly normal to read a lot," she said.

"Do you?" Sarah rolled her eyes. "But, Dr. Samson, if you call her when she's reading, if you say, 'Mum, it's dinnertime. Now put that book away!' she doesn't even answer!"

And good luck to her, thought Marigold, though all she said was "Mmm," before changing the subject smoothly. "So … this holiday?" she asked, nodding toward the shiny brochures in Mousie's lap.

"My sister said she might be able to take her," Sarah whispered nervously, her eyes swerving toward her mother-in-law and then back again to Marigold. "It's only a 'might' because Marjorie's a bit scared of her—Mum can be quite sharp-tongued, you know. Comes from all those years of being a teacher—"

"Does it?" said Marigold.

"So—so we're not sure yet if we'll be going," said Sarah, and she looked down at the glossy brochures and sighed, the tiniest, saddest sigh that Marigold had ever heard, and one that ordinarily would have been the signal for her to say, "Look, if you can't find anyone, and it's only for a few days, your mother-in-law can stay with me …"

But she stayed guiltily silent; only last week she'd promised Lily she wouldn't bring any more lame ducks home. "It's not *professional*, Mum!" Lily was always pointing out. "And I'll tell you something else."

"What?

"You're going to get stuck one day." There'd been an edge of triumph in Lily's voice.

"Stuck?"

"Yes! One of those care-giver kids will go away and not come back, and you'll be left holding the oldie."

Marigold had laughed, a little uneasily. "Of course they won't."

"Of course they *would*. You're such a softie, Mum. Don't you read the papers?"

"I haven't got the time."

"Well, old people get abandoned every single day! Left on park benches! In railway stations! Without even a label around their neck to tell people who they are!"

There'd been a silence then. Marigold might not have time to read the paper every day, but she knew from her work that this was true.

"Promise me!" Lily had demanded.

"Promise what?" Marigold had asked, though indeed she'd known.

"That you won't bring any more lame ducks home—" Lily had paused to calculate, "—for at least a year."

A year and she would get out of the habit, that's what Lily had been thinking.

"But—"

"Mum, it's *unprofessional*!"

"Oh, all right." Marigold had given in.

A promise was a promise, so now she said briskly, smiling falsely at Sarah, "I'm sure it will work out, and the pair of you will be off on your lovely holiday," and though poor Sarah didn't seem to notice, Marigold thought her voice sounded false as well—brummy as a two-bob watch, as Pop would say.

4 NIGHTTIME

As Marigold drove down the highway toward home, the winter night began to close about the city. It crept down from the mountains where Nan and Pop lived, spreading an inky stain across the suburbs on the plain. Lights came on in the streets and houses, in Lily and Marigold's place and in Lonnie's Boarding House for Gentlemen, and in Mercer College, where, as the students returned, the windows lit up one by one until the residence hall was a tall bright tower against the darkened sky.

"Brummy as a two-bob watch," typed Clara Lee in her small room on the twentieth floor. Clara was writing her fourth-year thesis on Australian slang. "Flash as a rat with a gold tooth," she typed, and smiled. Now, wasn't that a kind of poetry?

Her dad wouldn't have agreed. Her dad had wanted her to study medicine instead of arts. Medicine was what he'd wanted to study when he'd been young, only his elderly parents had forced him to do accounting instead.

"I want to study what I *like*," Clara had insisted, almost adding, "I don't want to end up like you!"

Her dad had given in, though he'd started up again when she'd begun her thesis.

"If you're doing literature, why not choose something proper?"

"Proper?"

"Something … poetic." As he spoke the word, a faint flush had risen to her father's sallow cheeks. And no wonder, thought Clara, for her dad was the least poetic person you could imagine; it was even possible he didn't possess a soul.

"Poetic?" she'd said again, teasingly. There was a boy in her Lit Tut who looked poetic, tall and pale and thin, with a lock of long fair hair that fell across his forehead. His name was Lonnie Samson.

Her father had cleared his throat. "Something like Shakespeare, for instance, or the Romantic poets."

"But Dad, the kind of language I'm studying *is* poetic. Listen to this: *Cold as a stepmother's breath* … See?"

Her father hadn't seen. He'd kept on nagging and trying to boss her around. Clara didn't have to take it. She had her scholarship—she didn't have to live at home. She had left. There was nothing to it; you simply tossed your clothes in a bag and walked straight out the door. Easy.

Clara's fingers stilled on the keys. An image of her mother's face rose up: her soft brown eyes, that little tremble at the corner of her mouth when she got upset and didn't want you to know. "No," said Clara. "No. Go away, Mum." She shook her head sternly and banished Mum and then slowly began to type again.

In the room next door Clara's friend Jessaline O'Harris was checking through her notes for a test the next day. Every word she read made her feel sick. She hated Linguistics, hated it, hated it, hated it. Tears formed in her eyes, and her thick glasses steamed up. She chucked the heavy folder on the floor and reached for the book her friend Mrs. Murphy had loaned her that afternoon. Mrs. Murphy was in charge of the kitchens in Mercer College, and the book was *The Alice B. Toklas Cook Book.*

"I think you'll enjoy this, dear," Mrs. Murphy had said, and Jessaline knew she would, because she loved cooking and she loved reading about cooking. Even a simple list of ingredients could hold her spellbound. Yet as Jessaline opened the book to Chapter Seven ("Treasures"), her gaze flicked nervously toward the door, as if she expected her parents—two tall slope-shouldered academics with big round heads—to burst in and demand to know why she was reading cookbooks instead of studying for her exam. Jessaline felt her parents knew every single thing she was doing even before she did it. She felt they could read her mind.

Suddenly she remembered they were both away at a conference in Armidale. Clutching *Alice B. Toklas* to her chest, she sprang up from her desk and threw herself onto the bed. She snuggled back against the pillows and began to read: *A Hen With Golden Eggs/ Put a hen in a saucepan over very high heat. It should be covered with cold water, and when it is about to boil ...*

In his room at Mrs. Rasmussen's Boarding House for Gentlemen, Lonnie was reading, too. His book was a biography of his favorite writer, Emily Brontë, and the further he read, the more convinced he was that if Emily Brontë had been his contemporary, alive and young and studying at the university, he'd have fallen in love with her. But would she have returned the feeling?

Somehow Lonnie knew she wouldn't have: he could imagine her gaze on him, stern and clear-eyed, a little like his sister Lily's. She'd gaze, and turn away, something that seemed to happen with girls Lonnie fancied, not at first, but after a little while. "It's the way you toss back your hair," Lily had informed him once, "that long bit that falls over your forehead. There's a boy at school who has hair like yours, and he tosses it back—but only once, Lon. You keep on doing it and doing it, as if you haven't got the *strength*. It makes you look like one of those nodding toys people keep in the backs of their cars. It makes you look lacking."

"Lacking? Lacking in what?"

"Just lacking," Lily had replied.

The night grew deeper. The lights in Mercer College went out one by one, and the tall tower darkened and merged into the sky. Clara slept soundly and so did Jessaline, Clara's parents lay awake and thought about her, old Mrs. Nightingale sat up all night and read the poems of Robert Burns. *Wee, sleekit, cow'rin, tim'rous beastie,/ O, what a panic's in thy breastie!* she read, smiling to herself and thinking how very exactly Burns's description of a mouse fitted her poor daughter-in-law.

Lily turned and twisted beneath her covers, dreaming anxious little thoughts of shopping lists and overdue bills and a washing machine that kept on breaking down. One slender arm hung outside the covers, growing colder, and the small movement she made to draw it back into the warmth half woke her. And in that strange enchanted landscape between consciousness and sleeping, a face hovered—the face of Daniel Steadman, whom the girls in Year Ten had voted most handsome guy in Year Eleven. They hadn't used the word *handsome*—*tasty* was what they'd said, which Lily hated. It made him sound like a meal or some kind of snack waiting to be devoured. Or—"Whatever," Lily murmured, sleep closing

25

in on her fast. "Whatever—" Daniel Steadman was nothing to do with her; she doubted he'd ever even noticed her.

Up in the mountains, her nan and pop were dreaming, too. In their dreams they were very young: May was in the Girls' Home where she'd grown up, and her best friend Sef sat on the edge of her bed and whispered, "One day we'll have a celebration." May was so little she didn't know what *celebration* meant, though she thought it had the sound of bells. "Bells," she said in her sleep, out loud, so that beside her, Pop grunted and turned over, and falling deeper into sleep, he heard his mother's voice quite plainly. "Stanley? Stanley?"

"Yeah."

"I want you to mow the lawn tomorrow. It's getting out of hand."

"But tomorrow's *Saturday*. I was goin' down the creek with—"

"No buts, Stanley. I want that lawn done first thing, do you hear?"

Stanley grumbled and turned over again. "Yeah, I hear," he muttered, and then he woke and sat straight up in bed. It suddenly came to him that he couldn't remember the color of his mother's eyes.

5 THE WEDDING DRESS

In the morning, though he had no memory of his mother's voice from his dream of the night before, Lily's pop decided it was time to mow the lawn—there'd been a mild spell the week before, and the grass, dormant all through winter, had begun to grow again. "Spring's on the way," he said to May, and besides, he had a spanking brand-new mower he was eager to try out.

"A *new* mower, Pop?" Lily had exclaimed when he'd mentioned it on the telephone, and her voice had been incredulous, as if Stan had proposed something young and outrageous, like getting his navel pierced or paddling a plastic bathtub down the Amazon. "But, Pop, why do that? Why not get someone to come in and mow the lawn for you?"

Stan loved Lily, and since he'd written off her hopeless brother, she was his only grandchild. All the same, when she'd suggested he get someone in to do the mowing, a small spurt of rage had flared hotly up against his ribs. She thought he was past it! He could hear it in her voice. Past mowing a bit of grass himself! Past buying a new mower! A new mower, which, at his age, Lil obviously thought would be a waste because he'd have kicked the bucket before it was broken in! It was as painful as the time his daughter Marigold had suggested he and May get Meals on Wheels. Meals on Wheels! What did she think they were? Even gentle May had protested: "Why, Marigold! Meals on Wheels is for *old* people!"

27

They hadn't gotten Meals on Wheels. May still did the cooking, and they managed their own shopping up at the Safeway every Saturday afternoon. And Stan had bought his mower and found a place for it in the shed because you couldn't leave a brand-new mower, with its optimistic scents of fresh oil and spanking brand-new paint to rust away in the damp air of the mountains, the mist that May always called—after a song a childhood friend had taught her—the foggy, foggy dew.

The shed was crowded with all the bits and pieces of their earlier lives. May couldn't throw a thing away if it might hold some old memory, so boxes and barrels lined the walls, cases were stacked in the corners, and odd bits of furniture took up the center space: a worn old sofa from their first house in Fivedock, a set of kitchen chairs, their daughter Marigold's old cot, a battered wardrobe with a tricky door Stan had never been able to fix. Now, as he tugged at the mower, the tricky door swung open, and he saw the trunk inside: a small trunk, which had the familiarity of an object once known but long forgotten. Mum's, was it? His sister Emmy's?

Mum's. Yeah, it was Mum's old trunk, sent on to him when his sister Emmy had passed away. Stan had never opened it, never even touched the thing. How could he? It had been hard enough to believe that Emmy had died; stout, loud-voiced Emmy who'd bossed him all through childhood—how could such a noisy person actually be dead?

Stan didn't know what made him do it now; he abandoned the glossy new mower, dragged the old trunk from the wardrobe, knelt down on the cold cement floor and forced the rusty catches, flung back the lid, and peered inside.

He found paper. Clouds of it. Layer on layer of filmy tissue, so old the colors had turned milky, the paper gone limp and soft as cloth. "Twenty-six, twenty-seven," counted Stan, as the sheets sighed beneath his fingers until pinned to the twenty-eighth and last sheet he found a note on the blue-lined paper Emmy had always used. "Mum's Wedding Dress," he read. He lifted the sheet, and wisps of dried lavender and ancient rose petals floated into the air.

There it was, then.

And Stan remembered it, even though he'd seen the dress only once before, on the evening Emmy had come home and announced that she and Brian Kelloway were engaged, and Mum had brought this dress out from some secret hiding place and shown it to them, holding it up against the light. "My wedding dress," she'd said shyly, smiling at the pair of them. "Emmy, perhaps you—"

"I can't wear that! " Emmy had protested. "It looks like a nightie!"

"A nightie!" Stan had echoed, giggling wildly, jumping up and down so that the old floorboards had shivered and the pots rattled on the stove. He'd been ten at the time, and you didn't know what was what at that age.

And though it was all of seventy years ago, he could remember how his mother's face had gone bright red. They were all like that, he and Mum and Emmy—when they were hurt or angry, the skin of their faces turned a dark, dull red. They couldn't do anything about it; everyone could see how they felt. Lily was like that, too.

Back then, Stan hadn't noticed how Mum was hurt because they were poking fun at her wedding dress, and neither had Emmy, though Em had been eighteen. He could only see it now, when he was eighty and Mum and Emmy were gone; he could see Mum's stubby fingers folding the dress away, hear her voice saying stiffly, "Well, it's not a nightie." He could even hear her footsteps on the hall linoleum bearing it away.

He'd never seen it again.

Stan lifted the dress carefully from the trunk. The soft white—silk, was it? he didn't know much about fabric—had mellowed to a creamy color over years and years. It was older than he was, older by a good twenty years: a dress going on for its centenary. There was fancy stuff along the top and down along the hem—wide bands of tiny pearly beads in the shapes of leaves and flowers. Stan thrust out a stubby finger, half expecting the beads to fall at his touch and scatter on the oily floor of the shed, but they held fast, and he thought how things were made properly in those days, made to last. Folding the wedding dress across his arms, he carried it out from the shed.

It was a gloomy morning up there in the mountains, the clouds hung low, and the foggy dew drifted in fat white streamers across the yard, and yet as Stan crossed the lawn toward the back door, there was such a feeling of warmth on his arms where he held the dress that he thought for a moment the sun had come out, and he looked up in surprise.

There was no sun. It was the dress; it was like carrying a warm ray of sunlight folded across his arms.

"Emmy thought it looked like a nightie," he told May.

"A nightie? Nonsense!" May took the dress from Stan's arms and laid it gently over the back of the sofa, its soft length spilling down over the plumped cushions and ribbed blue corduroy. "It's a 1920s wedding dress, anyone can see."

"Yeah, well, I don't know about that—dresses and stuff."

"And your Emmy wouldn't have fitted inside it anyway." May giggled. "She was a big old thing. Same here—" May patted her ample hips. "It wouldn't have fitted me either, or our Marigold. You need to be skinny for this kind of dress. A chemise dress, it's called." May's voice went soft on the word *chemise,* as if she'd remembered her own mother in just such a dress—scoop-necked, sleeveless, and embroidered—leaning over the cot to scoop May up in her arms. That couldn't be, of course, because Lily's nan had been a foundling; she'd never known her mother.

Lily had been ten when she'd learned Nan had been brought up in a children's home, and for a long time afterward she'd kept waking up in the middle of the night, imagining what it might feel like to be all by yourself in the world. Not simply to be without a dad, but to have absolutely no one in your family: no Mum or Dad, no brothers and sisters or uncles and aunties and cousins, no Nan or Pop—no one except for you. And though she lay snug beneath her duvet, the thought would make Lily go cold all over, from the top of her head to the tips of her tingly toes. To have *no one.* It made her own small family, with all its faults and peculiarities, its bickerings and squabblings, seem rich in comparison.

It certainly seemed rich to May. In her pretty living room, she gazed tenderly at the wedding dress and dreamily ran a finger along its beaded hem. "Look at this embroidery, Stan— the work in *that!* Think she did it herself? Your mum?"

"Dunno." Stan felt a small stab of guilt, because shouldn't he know something like that about his mum? He remembered her sitting out on the front veranda on summer evenings passing him a needle and a length of dull gray cotton. "Thread this for me, will you, love? My eyes aren't what they used to be." Patches on his school shorts, that had been, and beside her chair lay a skirt of Emmy's with its hem to be let down. No embroidery, though—bringing up two kids on a widow's pension wouldn't have left much time for fancywork. But perhaps when she was younger, before she'd married …

"They're lilies," said May, tracing the pattern of tiny beads. "Little lilies. See, Stan? If she did it herself, they must have been her favorite flowers. Were they?"

"Can't remember," Stan kicked at the carpet, feeling guilty again.

"And now we've got a Lily in the family! Your mum would have loved that, I bet." May's face lit up. "Wouldn't it be wonderful if Lily could wear this dress on her wedding day!"

Stan eyed the dress, and snorted. "More like a miracle, if you ask me."

"What?" May was indignant. "Our Lily's a lovely girl! "

"Didn't mean that."

"Then what did you mean?"

Stan jabbed a thumb at the dress. "Lil's the wrong shape."

May studied the dress for a moment, picturing her granddaughter. She hated to admit it, but Stan was right: Lily wasn't big, but she was stocky, square-shaped, like Stan—the dress wouldn't fit across her shoulders, for a start. A shadow of disappointment crossed May's face. She would have loved to pass this dress on within the family, to see it worn at another wedding. Suddenly she brightened; "Lonnie!" she exclaimed.

Stan frowned. "What's he got to do with it?"

Even to hear his grandson's name made Stan's face turn red. Lon had done his dash with Stan.

"When he gets married," explained May.

Stan glowered. "Wearing frocks now, is he?"

"Of course not," said May. "And what if he was? But I meant his bride."

"His *bride?* Who the heck would want to marry Lonnie?"

"Lots of girls," said May stoutly.

"They'd have to be a shingle short then," said Stan. "And we don't want another loony in the family. Lon's enough for us."

"There's nothing wrong with Lonnie."

Stan ignored this. "Reckon you're behind the times anyway," he said in a superior tone. "They don't get married these days."

"Sometimes they do," retorted May, but Stan didn't hear her. Turning on his heel, he stomped out of the room. The back door banged and then creaked open again.

May went out and closed it. "Born in a tent!" she observed, inclining her head a little, as if she was speaking to someone standing beside her. She went back into the living room and sat down on the sofa, patting the cushion next to her as if inviting another person to sit down. She lifted the dress onto her lap and stroked its creamy folds.

"Beautiful, isn't it?" she said. "Don't you think so, Sef?"

6 ELECTRIC JUG

"Consider:" wrote Lily, copying down Mr. Skerrit's Friday discussion topic from the board, "if Hamlet was a teenager, how would this affect your view of Shakespeare's play?"

A lot, thought Lily, imagining Hamlet with her brother's melancholy face and that low, tragic voice she'd heard from her room those nights long ago when she'd been in Year Six and Lonnie had been studying for his SAT exam. Lonnie muttering quotations and statistics as he paced up and down the hall, Lonnie telling Mum he was convinced he was going to fail, Mum crying, "No, no! Of course you won't!" which would have been encouraging except for that fearful little quiver in her voice that meant she was as scared as he was.

Lonnie's SAT exam was long behind him. He'd passed it—just. Gone on to University, kept dropping out and dropping in again. He was twenty-two now, no longer a teenager, and yet his habits were teenaged—and Lily could easily imagine Hamlet having these habits: lying in bed all weekend brooding about himself, using three towels to take a shower, and leaving them lying in a wet clump on the bathroom floor for someone else to pick up. Leaving the electric heater on all night instead of switching it off when he went to bed …

Switching it off—a disturbing thought struck Lily: had she turned off the electric jug before she left home this morning? She pictured the dark little kitchen at home, the wooden bench beside the sink, and the big electric jug, which sat square in the middle of it, a jug so ancient that it didn't switch off automatically—you had to turn it off at the wall. And Lily couldn't remember if she'd done that this morning. She remembered putting it on after Mum had left for work, thinking she'd have a second cup of tea, and then realizing she simply didn't have the time.

But had she turned the jug off then?

Lily screwed her eyes shut, trying to remember.

"Something wrong, Lily?" asked Mr. Skerrit jovially. "Sight of a bit of homework too much for you?"

"Oh no," said Lily. "It wasn't that." Jolted so abruptly from her anxious reverie, she almost added, "I can't remember if I turned the jug off," and stopped herself just in time. How ridiculous she would have sounded! How stodgy, how middle-aged! A warm tide of color flooded her cheeks as she imagined the giggles and whispers rippling round the class.

Lily took up her pen again and tried industriously to make notes. "Can a person always be a teenager?" she scribbled. "Or always middle-aged? (Like me?) If Hamlet ..." But it was no good; the dark little kitchen slid into her mind again. What would happen if she had left the jug turned on?

First it would burn dry. Then what? The coils inside the jug would grow red hot, and then the jug itself; the old wooden bench would blacken, begin to smoke, to flare; the curtains at the window would catch, and then the wall—their poor old house would burn and—and how pleased Pop would be! "Now you can buy a place that's fit for human habitation!"

The bell rang for the end of first period. Second period was Library, easy to skip because Ms. Esterhazy hardly ever bothered with the roll. Lily's house (if it was still there) was three short streets away. She could be home and back before anyone would notice she was gone.

The jug sat on the bench, stone cold. She'd run home for nothing, and now she felt a fool, a stupid, middle-aged fool. Sitting with Tracy Gilman and the other girls at lunch and recess, Lily could take part in their conversations; she could *sound* like them, she knew the words: *gross* and *glam* and *fave* and *juicy*—yet inside, where it mattered, Lily felt a fraud. When Tracy went on about some boy she fancied, or poor Lizzie Banks wondered aloud if that dimply skin on her thighs could possibly be cellulite, what Lily really felt like saying was: "Tsk," the little sound Nan made when the milk boiled over or when Pop left a trail of muddy footprints on the newly polished floor. And "Tsk" wasn't even middle-aged—it was old. Even her mother never said it.

What's *happening* to me? wondered Lily, her gaze traveling around the kitchen, over the grotty old bench and down the cupboard doors, and then very slowly across the old linoleum, as if the answer to her question might lie inscribed in those mysteriously faded patterns she and Lonnie had never been able to work out. Were they leaves and flowers? Baskets? Clouds and unicorns?

Oh! Lily gave a small startled jump. In the dark corner by the sink, beneath the hole in the skirting board that had been there for ages, Lily saw something pale and lifeless lying, something pudgy, huddled …

"Seely?" she whispered.

Seely was the name of a hamster Lonnie had owned, way back when he was in Grade Six and Lily had just been starting school. Seely had disappeared, and Lonnie had claimed, *still* claimed, even now, that those mysterious scuttlings in their walls at night were made by Seely, an old, old Seely, perhaps with a wife, and children.

Lily took a cautious step toward the corner. Could Lonnie have been right? Could this huddled shape be Seely, perhaps come out to die? Seely had been that exact shade of dirty, brownish gray. Seal-gray. How long did hamsters live?

"Seely?" Lily whispered again, prodding the small still shape gently with her shoe. How creepily it sort of *gave*. Changed shape, became long and limp and raggy so she saw at once it was nothing more than the wet dishcloth that Mum, in a hurry to get to work, must have lobbed at the sink and missed, and then, like Lonnie, and possibly Hamlet, couldn't be bothered to pick up. Lily snatched it from the floor and hung it where it should be, on the hook above the sink. The faucet was dripping sullenly; it needed a new washer. She'd have to remember to buy one from the hardware store. "Tsk," she muttered irritably.

Tsk? *Just like Nan.*

Lily scowled. It was being the sensible one of the family that was making her act like this, filling her mind with cooking and shopping and electric jugs. Something had to be done before it was too late—something totally impractical and nonsensible, the kind of action no one would expect from her. Like what?

Stop helping Mum with the housework? She pictured her mother's tired face and knew that couldn't be done. Run off like Lonnie? Fat chance!

Outside, the sun came out. A gleam pierced through the ivy at the window and made a pool of light upon the floor. The old fridge hummed and spluttered and mercifully began to hum again. Fall in love, thought Lily suddenly. Tracy and Lizzie and Lara were always in love with someone or about to be or falling out of love, hopeful and eager, then radiant and happy, then crying, then hopeful all over again. What could be less sensible than that? Fall in love, then. But with whom?

An image of Daniel Steadman swam into Lily's mind: straight black hair brushed back from his forehead, eyes so deeply blue they made you shiver. Why had she thought of *him?* She didn't know him, and he most certainly didn't know her. Distantly she heard the school bell sound for recess. With one last disgusted glance around the kitchen, Lily headed for the door.

The sun in the streets lifted her spirits. The gloom that had descended on her began to seep away. She hadn't had enough sleep last night, that was all. She'd had dreams, the disturbing kind you couldn't remember when you woke but that left a kind of feeling over the day. Of course she wasn't middle-aged! And there was nothing wrong with being sensible. Fall in love? Start thinking about some boy you didn't even know? Idiotic, thought Lily. Ridiculous!

Just what she needed, then.

Wasn't it?

No, decided Lily. As if she didn't have enough troubles.

But ten minutes later, as she hurried down the corridor toward the Art Room, she saw Daniel Steadman turning into the senior common room. As she passed, their eyes caught—it was only for a second, but the tiny encounter gave Lily a strange light, woozy feeling inside her head: it made her brain feel funny, like a … like a tablet fizzing, dissolving away inside a water glass.

She wasn't sure she liked the sensation.

7 NO GRANDSON OF MINE

Up in the mountains, Stan was still in a temper. He strode around the yard, his face bright red, his black eyes glinting fiercely beneath his bristly brows. Why did May have to bring Lonnie's name into every single conversation? Attach it to the most unlikely subjects, like Mum's old wedding dress, when she knew, because he'd told her, as he'd told Lonnie and the rest of the family, that Lonnie was no grandson of his anymore.

Stan kicked at the trunk of an apple tree. He knew why she did it. Of course he did—there were no flies on him: May wanted him to make up with Lonnie; she'd never been able to stand quarrels and fights within the family. Stan clenched his fists inside his pockets. This time she'd have to put up with it; he wasn't giving in.

Not that May herself would give up easily; she was stubborn, too. A few nights back she'd waited until he was asleep and then nudged him awake. She'd wanted to know if he remembered Lonnie back when he was five, the time his dad had left, and still half asleep, Stan hadn't been able to fight off a sudden sharp image of a bony little head dug urgently into his ribs. "'Course I do," he'd answered and then turned over and pretended to fall asleep again.

So what if Lon's dad had left? What about Lily, then? The shifty hippie bugger had left before she was even born, and Lily was all right. Lily was doing fine. And didn't that sort of thing happen in every second family these days? Hadn't Stan's own dad died of flu when Stan was only seven? You got over things; you had to. You knuckled down. Only Lonnie never had. "And never *will*," Stan muttered furiously. Lon had been a clever little kid—you could see it in his eyes—and yet he'd never done a stroke of work at school, passed each year by the skin of his teeth and then gone off to Tafe to do some kind of creative writing course and dropped out halfway through. "The only thing I learned," he'd told Stan, "was that I don't have any talent, Pop."

"You didn't stay there long enough to learn even that much," Stan had growled.

Next, Lonnie had found a job at some fancy plant place decorating malls and the foyers of big hotels—two months and he'd chucked that; then off to horticultural college. Only that didn't suit him either—"You have to learn the names of eight hundred and fifty types of plants, Pop, and I haven't got the memory."

Stan had exploded. "You're twenty years old, and you don't have a memory! I'm going on eighty, and I've got one. Your grandmother's over seventy, and she can remember the name of every girl in her first class at primary school!"

"But that's *people*, Pop."

"Eh?"

"People's different. I can remember *people*—it's facts I'm bad about. Lists and stuff. Plants, Pop. They're just names to me. There's nothing you can get a grip on."

"Get a grip on yourself! What are you going to do now?"

"No worries, Pop."

No worries. How Stan hated that phrase.

"I'll think of something," said Lonnie cheerfully.

He'd thought of Economics at the university. Economics hadn't worked out either. Soulless, Lonnie had said. Soulless! That boy always had a word for it—he could talk through wet cement.

And yet, visiting at Marigold's house, Stan was disturbed by his grandson's appearance. His face looked downright old. Dark blue circles hung beneath his eyes, and his skin had a waxy sheen. The long hair that fell from a center parting clear down past his shoulders, that dull lank lock across his forehead seemed lighter, seemed—

"Are you going gray?" demanded Stan.

"Gray?"

"Your hair."

"It's streaks, Pop. Silver streaks."

Silver *streaks*!

Lonnie had dropped out of Economics two weeks later.

The crisis had occurred last summer—on the long weekend when the family had come to visit. Now it was Marigold who was looking under the weather: pale and drawn, her eyes red-rimmed as if she'd lain awake all night. "Something wrong?" Stan had asked her.

They were in the garden, on the bench beneath the jacaranda. From there you could see the whole of the valley and the hills rising up beyond it, layer on layer of blue. Nearer to home, you could see the shady corner down at the bottom of the yard where the two apple trees grew, the summer hammock hung between them, Lonnie swinging slowly in it, one delicate white foot drooping, white toes brushing the long green grass.

"Marigold?" Stan prompted, because she hadn't replied. A single tear rolled down her cheek. Stan had jerked a thumb toward the hammock. "It's him, isn't it?" Of course it was. "What's he done now?"

Marigold turned and flung herself against his chest. "Dad, I can't stand it anymore!"

Of course she couldn't. Neither could he. "You mean the way he keeps on dropping out?"

"No," she'd said sadly. "I've gotten used to that. It's the way he keeps on starting up again. He's talking about doing Arts now, and I *dread* it, Dad. Because when he starts on something, I know, three months down the track, he's going to—"

"Right."

It was at this point that Stan had gone for the ax, the shiny new one he'd bought to deal with the lantana down back. He'd run, yes, despite his almost eighty years, he'd run to the shed and grabbed it, and then, holding the smooth wooden handle behind his back, he'd crept stealthily down to the hammock where that slender white foot still dangled lazily in the grass.

"Starting another course, are you?"

Lonnie looked up and favored his grandpa with a calm, mild smile. "Yeah, Pop. English Lit. You know, I think this might be *me*, Pop."

"Might it?"

"Yeah."

"How old are you now, Lon? Twenty-one?"

"Twenty-two."

"Twenty-two, eh? When I was your age, I'd been pounding a copper's beat for four bloody years."

"Yeah, I know, Pop. But—"

"But what?"

"It was a different world then, Pop." There was a kind of lazy patronage in Lonnie's voice, as if the world Stan had struggled through back in his own youth was simple and uncomplicated, a kindergarten sort of place.

"Now listen here—"

"And I'm a different kind of person from you," Lonnie went on smoothly.

"That so?"

Lonnie smiled again. "Yeah."

Stan had begun to shout. "Take your bloody course, okay? Go on and take it! But if you drop it, if, if you—" his voice stumbled, recovered,"—you chuck it in, again, if you upset your mother one more time—"

"Mum doesn't mind," said Lonnie confidently. "She's used to it."

Stan drew the ax out from behind his back and raised it. A glint of sunlight dazzled along its edge.

"Geez!" Lonnie was out of the hammock now, edging back, alarmed. Stan had never seen him move so fast. "You wouldn't!"

"Just try me," said Stan.

"But—"

"No buts." Stan's voice was weary suddenly. "Just—get out of here! Give your mother a weekend without you! Give us all a break! Hop it to the station, okay?" Stan looked at his watch. "If you get a move on, you might just make the 4:30." He took a fifty from his wallet. "Here's your fare."

Lonnie drew himself up then. "I've got money," he said. "I work, Pop. I work part-time, at night, stacking shelves, I told you …"

"Just get," said Stan.

Stan hadn't seen him since, though he occasionally heard news from Marigold or May. Lonnie had started his course.

He'd moved out of home. He'd found himself a room in some kind of boarding house, over Toongabbie way—full of bed-bugs, probably. Lonnie wouldn't know what they were; he'd think he had a rash. Well, so what? Stan shook his head furiously as he circled the lawn again. He didn't care if the kid got himself eaten alive; he'd written him off. Lonnie was no grandson of his anymore.

Lonnie had done his dash, this time. You could bet your bottom dollar on that. Stan would not be moved.

Inside the house, May was dreaming of weddings; weddings in churches with bridesmaids and flower girls, organ music, and a choir singing. And afterward, long tables on a green lawn, crisp white tablecloths, strawberries and fresh cream, champagne, and flowers everywhere. And a bride in a wedding dress …

There'd been a dearth of wedding dresses in May's life. She herself had been married in the austere years just after the war, in a navy two-piece suit she'd saved for on coupons and a tiny little hat with a touch of violet veiling to match her eyes. As for Marigold—well, May had never known what kind of dress Marigold had worn because she and Stan hadn't been invited to the wedding. On the single occasion they'd met Oliver Dezoto, Marigold's fiancé, Stan had called him a name that even now could bring a flush of color to May's cheeks—and that had been that.

"What kind of wedding do you think it was?" she'd asked Stan sorrowfully on that long-ago day, for their daughter had told them the date, even though they weren't invited, and May hadn't been able to stop thinking of it all through the long afternoon.

"Bloody hippie drug-fest, love," Stan had replied. "You haven't missed a thing. And if I'd known the exact time and place, I'd have organized a raid."

All bluff, May had thought, because she knew Stan felt as hurt as she did.

"What do you think she wore?"

"Bloody gunny sack."

They needed a wedding in the family, May thought now. Well, they needed *some* kind of celebration. She'd given up on Marigold marrying again. "No *way*," said Marigold. "Marriage solves nothing, Mum," and she'd forbidden her mother to speak of the subject again.

And Lily vowed she wasn't getting married until she was at least forty. "There's a whole *world* out there, Nan!"

As for Lonnie, he was a dear good boy at heart, but the right girl would have to come along, and that might take some time—most things in Lonnie's life seemed to require time.

May sighed. "Not a wedding, then," she said to Sef, "at least not for a while."

Then she blushed, as if someone had caught her talking to her friend, as Marigold had often done when she was growing up. "Talking to yourself, Mum?" Marigold would say. "First sign of madness, that."

"Not to myself," May had replied. "To Sef."

"Sef? Who's Sef?"

"My—" May had grasped a phrase from the air and been stuck with it ever since. "My imaginary companion."

"Imaginary companion!" Marigold had scoffed. "Mum, act your age."

Sef wasn't imaginary. Sef had been quite real once upon a time, the big girl who'd looked after May back there in the children's home: Sef in her long white nightdress sitting on the edge of May's bed, holding her hand and chasing the bad dreams away, Sef's quick fingers braiding May's hair in the mornings, doing her buttons up right. "All long ago, now," May said, sighing, and folding Stan's mother's wedding dress across her arm, she got up from the sofa and went to the window. There was Stan still pacing around the garden, still brooding about Lonnie—she could tell by the stiff tilt of his head, the anger in his stride, the way he'd forgotten all about the mowing. As she watched, he stopped and stared out toward the hills, into the mist, the swirling clouds of foggy dew. There was a little stoop to those square shoulders now. Like her, he wasn't getting any younger; he'd be eighty in September.

Eighty! May drew in a quick, excited breath. Eighty was special, surely. She'd have a party for him! Not a big one, like her grandchildren's weddings would be—this would be just family and perhaps a few old friends. In September the garden would be at its loveliest—the lawn a pure bright green, the early roses out, the wisteria round the patio. It would be warm enough to have the table on the lawn and the white embroidered tablecloth Stan's mother had given them at their wedding, and she'd have streamers and floaty white balloons and fairy lights strung through the trees.

"A celebration," she said to Sef, and there was a kind of familiarity to the word, as if someone had said it to her very recently. "A celebration," she repeated, and now it seemed to her that the word had the sound of bells in it. And if there was a celebration, then Lonnie would have to come. He and Stan would make up. Of course they would. May's soft face took on a determined expression. She would make sure they did.

8 LONNIE'S TUTORIAL

Powdery golden sunlight drifted through the long windows of Dr. Finch's tutorial room, warming Lonnie's knees through the frayed denim of his jeans and his skinny arms through the loose weave of the big yellow sweater Nan had knitted for him. Lonnie basked in the sunshine; it actually seemed peculiar to feel warm again. Mrs. Rasmussen's Boarding House for Gentlemen was so cold that the small electric heater he'd picked up from the Op Shop barely made a dent in the deep freeze of his room. Lying in bed at night, Lonnie often pictured the small sitting room at home, its gas fire blazing, Lily doing her homework at the table, his mother deep in paperwork she'd brought home from her job, occasionally chatting with a lame duck she'd brought home as well.

Unlike Lily, Lonnie had never minded Mum's lame ducks in the house. These days, though, it gave him a twinge to think of one of them snuggled up warmly on the battered sofa, which had been his special place, and even sleeping in his bed in the small room down the hall.

Lonnie sighed and shifted, tipping his head back to let the sun shine on his face, stretching his long legs out so that he was almost lying in the chair. When he thought of home these days, it felt as if he'd been cast out, and yet he knew it hadn't really been like that. Pop might have thrown him out of *his* house, but Mum hadn't chucked him out of theirs. It had been his own choice to go; he'd wanted space from them.

All of them, not just Pop—Pop who thought he was useless, who said Lonnie had done his dash with him, whatever that meant. What was a dash? Lonnie closed his mind against the image of Pop's red angry face and a much older memory of a big warm hand enclosing his. Pop had done his dash with *him*. "He's no grandpa of *mine*," he muttered, and he didn't notice how the girl in the chair next to his turned her head and smiled.

Yeah, he'd wanted space from all of them: from Mum, who was always worrying about him and therefore made him worry about himself, from his bossy little sister who was just like Pop, and who thought he was useless, too, and even from Nan, who seemed to think he was some kind of angel fallen down from heaven, which somehow made Lonnie feel worst of all. They mucked you up; you didn't know who you were. He had to get himself sorted out. He had to work out what to do—but now the unaccustomed warmth took hold of Lonnie, his eyelids fluttered, and Dr. Finch's words on the poetry of Thomas Hardy rumbled right over him, like tumbrels on the way to the guillotine. His head drooped. He dreamed that kind of dream where you seem to wake in the place you've fallen asleep; and there at the windows of the tutorial room Lonnie saw a tall dark-haired young woman in a long brown dress peering inside the room. He knew at once who it was: his favorite writer, Emily Brontë—he'd know her anywhere. And she seemed to know him, too, because she was gazing straight at him and beckoning.

Lonnie rose from his chair and floated through the window into a landscape of stones and rough dry grasses and banks of purple flowers. He could hear water bubbling over pebbles, and a small brown bird rose up from the grass and spiraled into the wide blue sky. "Emily!" he called, and the tall young woman striding along a little way ahead of him turned, her great somber eyes shining, the corners of her long mouth lifting into a smile. "See, she likes me!" Lonnie murmured joyously. "See, Emily Brontë likes me! She understands. And if *she* likes me, then—ow!" he broke off with a small sharp yip, because someone, someone right next to him, had pinched his arm. Hard. He woke to see a pair of eyes, darker than Emily's, beneath a glossy blue-black fringe and recognized the fourth-year girl who sat in on some of the first-year tutorials.

"What—what's up?" he floundered.

The girl rolled her eyes sideways, and Lonnie turned his head to find Dr. Finch standing beside his chair. "Ah, so you're with us again, Mr. Samson." He was holding Lonnie's essay, ten creased and tumbled sheets on the poetry of Emily Brontë fastened together with the lucky paper clip Lonnie had kept from primary school, from Mrs. Phipson's Grade Four class where he'd won a chocolate car for his project, "What I Want to Be." Lonnie had wanted to be a flying doctor. How sure he'd been of everything back then!

Lonnie flipped through the pages, avoiding the last one, where the grade would be. He knew it wouldn't be good; Dr. Finch's agitated handwriting, peppered with exclamation marks, glared at him from every margin, a NO!! in block letters had torn the corner of a page.

"Mr. Samson?"

Lonnie looked up; Dr. Finch was still standing over him. "Too personal, I'm afraid," he said. "Too much detail about the author's life—that page on the chair she died in, for instance ..."

"It was a sofa," said Lonnie. "A black horsehair sofa."

"Yes, well—" Dr Finch waved a hand dismissively. "Details like that aren't important, Mr. Samson. This isn't a pensioners' reading group."

"I know," said Lonnie, wishing it could have been. All at once, as if he was drowning, his life began to flash before his eyes in a series of little pictures: primary and high school, the writing course at Tafe, Horticultural School, Economics 1, the whole confusing struggle to find something he could be. Pop's angry face, Mum's anxious one—if only he *was* a pensioner, then surely they would let him be.

"Without an understanding of contemporary literary theory, Mr. Samson," Dr. Finch was saying, "I'm afraid you're not going to get very far."

"I don't want to get far," muttered Lonnie childishly.

"So be it," Dr. Finch said, turning away.

So be it. Lonnie felt a deep chill gather in his chest. "So be it" sounded sort of dangerous, even—lethal. Was it worse, pondered Lonnie, or better than the phrase so many other teachers had left him with? "It's up to you."

Lonnie thought it sounded worse.

9 CLARA LEE

Out in the corridor, the students checked their grades, something they'd been too proud to do in Dr. Finch's company. There was a rustling of pages, little moans and sighs and grumbles, and the occasional gasp of sheer surprised delight.

Lonnie had a C.

C was undistinguished. C was—he knew it—borderline.

And yet when he'd written that essay on Emily Brontë's poetry, Lonnie had felt it was so *right*. Each idea, each image and detail, had fallen into place so simply it was as if the essay had always existed, fully formed and perfect, in some happy, cloudless region of his mind—the same place his Grade Four project had come from, perhaps. Writing it, especially the piece on Emily's death, which Dr. Finch had so derided, Lonnie had felt he'd begun to find himself, at last.

Only he'd been wrong, it seemed, and now the familiar panic began to surge inside him, the panic that had sent him to the Admin buildings of two colleges to give up his course and try something else again. And this was the worst time because he'd felt at home with English Lit, but this feeling must also have been an illusion, like having a dad had been an illusion, a long, long time ago. Lonnie crumpled the pages in his hand and began to run, swerving around the little groups of students, on down the corridor, bursting through the door into the courtyard, along the path toward

Administration. Behind him a girl called out, "Hey!" Lonnie kept on running. She couldn't be calling him; he didn't really know any of the girls at this university.

"Hey!" The voice was right behind him now. Lonnie swung around and saw the dark-haired girl who'd woken him in the tutorial hurrying toward him down the path. "Hey, wait!" she called again.

Lonnie turned around and pointed to his chest. "Me?" he asked "Do you mean me?"

She nodded.

Clara had no clear idea why she'd run after this boy, the tall thin fair-haired boy who'd fallen asleep in class and whom she'd always thought looked poetic. Was it because of his soft, romantic looks, or was it the way he'd muttered in his sleep "You're no grandfather of mine"? Certainly that had struck a chord with Clara, because it was exactly the way she felt about her dad. "You're no dad of *mine!*" Or was it because he'd seemed so upset back there in the corridor, as if those crumpled pages of his essay had contained a death warrant instead of Dr. Finch's predictable disapproval? Perhaps he didn't know Dr. Finch never gave anyone a good mark if he could help it.

"Marked you down?" she asked him boldly.

"Yeah." Lonnie flushed and looked down. He saw her feet, the little red boots she wore. They looked like shoes from a fairy tale.

"I know it's none of my business ..." she began.

Lonnie raised his eyes. "Oh, it *is*," he said fervently, because he didn't want her to go.

"It is?" asked Clara, surprised. "You mean you don't mind my butting in?"

"Oh, *no.*" He flicked the long pale lock he'd once dyed silver from his forehead, and it fell right back again.

"Only you looked so upset back there, and perhaps, I thought—I mean you mightn't know Dr. Finch does it to *everyone,*" she said. "Marks them down, I mean."

"Does he?"

She nodded. "Especially if they're good."

Lonnie flushed. "I'm not good normally—except, just this once I thought I'd gotten it right, you know?"

She nodded.

"It made me feel like chucking it in."

"Oh, don't!" She sounded as if she really meant it, as if, for some strange reason, she'd like it if he stayed right here.

"It was only for a moment," he said airily, because he didn't want her to think he was a wimp. "Anyway, my pop would kill me if I dropped this course."

"Your dad?"

"Haven't got a dad. I mean, I did have, but he—left."

"Oh! Sorry!"

"It was ages back," said Lonnie, nonchalant this time. "I can hardly remember him."

And that was true, he thought, no matter that Lily disbelieved him. He couldn't remember Dad, except in random little flashes he was never sure about; the only thing he remembered properly was the feeling in the house after Dad had gone, as if he and Mum had been let loose into an empty sky. "Pop's my grandpa," he said. "He's got this ax, and he says he'll use it on me if I drop out anymore."

Clara laughed. "Oh, I bet he wouldn't," she said.

"He might, if he got mad enough."

The girl shook her head, eyes wide, and suddenly Pop's

hostility didn't seem to matter quite so much, and even the wasted essay wasn't so important, because Lonnie had the definite feeling he was going to do better next time round. He bounced on his toes; he felt strangely light, as if some heaviness had risen from inside him and floated away like the mist his nan called foggy dew.

He gazed at the girl. She was so small and slender, no bigger than those Grade Six girls who called out to him every time he walked past the primary school. She wore a pleated skirt and a long green sweater in a wool so fine and soft it made you long to touch it. When she blinked, her long black lashes swept against the warm curve of her cheek. Lonnie thought he'd never seen anything quite so lovely, unless it was her tiny feet in those fairy-tale red boots. "Um ..." he began.

"What?" She smiled at him.

"Fancy a coffee? Over at the Union?" He held his breath.

"Sure."

The thick lock of hair felt even heavier on his lightened forehead. He flicked it back; the lock fell forward again, hot and clammy against his skin. He flicked once more and then remembered Lily telling him the gesture made him seem what she called lacking.

Then something astonishing happened. Clara leaned forward and gently smoothed the stray lock of hair back from his hot forehead.

For a long moment they simply stood there. Then Clara held out her hand. "I'm Clara Lee," she said.

"Lonnie. Lonnie Samson."

His hand seemed to melt into hers.

10 DANIEL STEADMAN

Now that Lonnie had moved out, the house seemed extra lonely when Lily got home from school, especially on those winter evenings when the light began to fade at half past four.

"Mum!" she called, twisting her key in the lock, pushing the door open, stepping into the hall. "Mum!" There were some days, very rare days, when her mother got home before her.

Today wasn't one of them. Lily walked on down the hallway switching on the lights, her school shoes clumping on the dull scuffed floor, and when she kicked them off and dropped her schoolbag and sank down onto her bed, everything was silent and the cold air hummed inside her ears. Hollow, that was how their house felt now, and all at once she wondered if this was how it might have seemed to Lonnie after their dad had gone. The idea surprised her. She had never thought of Lonnie in this way—as a little kid whose dad had vanished, yet he'd been almost six at the time, which was surely old enough to feel abandoned. Old enough to miss someone, anyway—could that long-ago desertion even be the reason her brother was so hopeless? As if their father's leaving had left a hollowness not just inside the house but inside Lonnie, too?

It didn't seem so. "I can hardly remember him," Lonnie would say quickly, whenever Lily asked about their dad.

"What did he look like?" she'd ask, and then Lonnie would close his eyes, a pained expression gathering on his face.

"Why do you look like that?"

"I'm concentrating," Lon would say. "I'm trying to *remember.*" And then he'd put a hand up to his forehead—like a medium at a séance, Lily thought.

"He had a beard. And—" here Lonnie's fingers would twitch against his brow,"—and a long sort of face. Long cheeks—"

"Is that *all* ? You must remember more than that! You were nearly six! I can remember heaps of things from when I was six! What about your first day at school?"

"My first day at school?"

"Yes! Did he take you? Bring you back?"

"Mum did."

Lily would give up at this point. It was hopeless asking him anything.

"I can remember him," she'd said once.

"But you weren't even born!"

"Unborn babies can hear, can't they? Inside their mother's tummies? They can hear music, so why not voices? I can remember his voice."

"That's from the telephone," Lonnie had told her. "When he calls at Christmas and stuff. That's what you're remembering."

Lily was sure it wasn't. The voice in her memory was younger.

Now she went into her mother's room and took the old shoe box from the top shelf of the wardrobe. A shoe box! Proper families kept their photographs in albums, labeled with names and dates and places …

Lily sorted through them; there weren't many, no more than a handful, really. A small Lonnie in a party hat, at someone else's party. Lily as a baby in her mother's arms. And then in Nan's arms. Two-year-old Lily holding hands with Lonnie. Pop and Nan. School photos. No wedding photos. What kind of family had no wedding photos? Right at the bottom, she found the single photograph their mum had kept of their father.

Lonnie was right about the long cheeks. And the beard. Apart from that, the rest of him was—scrawny. Harmless, you'd think, looking at him. Inoffensive.

Pop hadn't thought so. "I knew he was no good the minute I set eyes on him!" Pop loved to say.

"The *only* time you saw him," Mum would retort.

"And that was enough. Eyes too close together, I spotted it at once. Shifty."

Was that true? wondered Lily. Were people with their eyes set close together shifty, never to be trusted? She put the photo back in the box and returned it to the wardrobe. Then she went into her own room, opened the drawer in her bedside table, and took out her copy of last year's school magazine. The pages fell open of their own accord, to page 53, where there was a photograph of the Drama Society, with Daniel Steadman in the middle of the back row.

Lily flopped down on her bed and gazed into Daniel's face. These last few days, ever since that morning in the kitchen when she'd said to herself, not meaning it, not serious at all, "I should fall in love," Lily had been haunted by the image of Daniel Steadman. It was the stupidest thing—she bent her head over the magazine, studying his face, trying to make out if his eyes were set too close together. It was hard to be sure—

there were so many kids in the photograph, and his face was so very tiny. All the same, she was almost certain the positioning of his eyes was normal. And they were such beautiful eyes, even in such a poor photograph, you could see. "Oh!" exclaimed Lily, impatient with what seemed to her a kind of airhead foolishness. How had she gotten like this? Only a week had passed since that morning in the kitchen when she'd thought about falling in love and then decided, out in the sunshine of the streets, that the idea was ridiculous, that she didn't need it. And yet it had happened, despite herself, as if a spell had been cast, some spirit conjured. Lily shivered, remembering that tiny corpselike shape in the corner of the room, the shape that had looked like Seely, or his ghost ...

Lily threw the magazine aside and crept out to the kitchen. It was strange how the empty house always made her creep, as if she was an intruder in someone else's home. She saw at once that the Seely-colored dishcloth wasn't hanging where it should be, on its hook; this time it lay curled in the soap dish on the edge of the sink, curled like a tiny creature fast asleep. Lily prodded at it cautiously; she felt only cold wet cloth, and the dark red splotch on its side that looked like fresh blood was only a stain of tandoori sauce from the chicken they'd had the night before. Lily took a fresh dishcloth from the drawer, thrust the old one into a plastic lunch bag, and took it outside to the bin.

It was a clear, still night—how long had she spent going through those photos, gazing at Daniel's face in the school magazine? Above their small back garden the stars blazed down, the very same stars that Daniel would see if he paused to look out of the window in the middle of his homework or wandered out into the garden for a breath of air. This thought made her feel close to him, as if she could reach out her hand and touch his. "Oh, *stop* it!" fumed Lily. "Stop thinking about him!"

But what did she do the very minute she got back to her room? Picked up the magazine, of course, still open at page 53, picked it up, and kissed the photograph.

Actually kissed it, before she could stop herself.

She could hardly believe she'd *done* that. "I've got a crush on Daniel Steadman," she whispered miserably, because it was so embarrassing, a *crush*, like some little girl in Year Seven. Ugh. The sort of thing that made your toes curl up inside your shoes. She'd wanted to stop feeling middle-aged, and she'd succeeded. She felt young now, only it was the wrong sort of young, like a very little kid who couldn't talk properly and kept falling off her bicycle.

"Daniel Steadman doesn't even know I exist," she said out loud and bracingly.

Of course he didn't. And yet it seemed to Lily now that when they passed each other in the corridors and playground there was a kind of tension between them. She couldn't tell whether the tension was desire or disgust. Or was she imagining the whole thing? Of course she was.

The phone shrilled out in the hall, and Lily tossed the magazine down on the bedside table and ran to answer. Oh, it was embarrassing, it was shameful—how when the phone rang she always thought it might be him. How could it be?

She picked up the receiver. "Hello," she said, listening tensely.

It was only Nan.

11 A CALL FROM NAN

"Lily?"

"Nan?"

"Yes, it's me, lovie. Lily, guess what?"

Lily was silent. How could you ever guess? Nan could call up to tell you her snowdrops were out in the bottom of the garden or her family of blue wrens had returned or that her friend Mrs. Petrie (a real friend, this one, not imaginary like Sef) had bought a pair of ducks. "Muscovy, dear."

"What's happened?" Lily asked her.

"You'll never believe what your pop's gone and done!"

Lily felt a tumbling sensation deep down in her stomach. She'd believe almost anything of Pop. Got himself arrested? she thought, though she didn't say it aloud to Nan. Perhaps there was some poor old lady up there in the hills, living in a shabby old house on valuable property that Pop had thoughtfully burned down so she could live in a nice new flat with all modern conveniences.

"What's he done?" she asked.

"He's gone and found his mum's wedding dress!" Nan told her. "In this old trunk down at the back of the shed."

"Pop had a *mum*?" It was something Lily could imagine only with the greatest difficulty, because it meant thinking of Pop as a little boy, and that was really hard to do. All she could manage was a shorter Pop, still red-faced and piggy-eyed, the kind of little kid who threw stones at girls and other people who weren't exactly like him: quiet boys with good manners, little old ladies, people who weren't Australian …

"Of course he had a mum!" Nan said indignantly. Then her voice softened. "Lily, that dress—it's so beautiful!"

"Oh," said Lily. Way back in primary school, she and her best friend Annabel had a passion for wedding dresses and weddings and brides. They'd waited outside churches on Saturday afternoons, spent whole Sundays cutting out brides' and bridesmaids' pictures from the old magazines Annabel's mum brought home from her job in the doctor's office. They'd designed their own wedding veils and dresses, chosen bridesmaids, and flowers for their brides' bouquets. "Oh, I can't *wait*, can you?" they'd whispered to each other. But that was long ago, Annabel and her family had moved away, and now Lily was in Year Ten, and she could see through all that kind of stuff: commercialism, that's all it was—

And yet, as Nan went on describing Pop's wedding dress, Lily couldn't stop a tiny sigh escaping from her lips. And that was because of her stupid crush on Daniel Steadman, of course; it was turning her soft—Lily shook her black curls wildly, to rid her head of all the soppy stuff that made you feel as if you weren't a real girl unless a boy noticed you.

"Lily?" The little voice crackled in her ear. "Lily, are you still there?"

"Yeah, Nan, I'm here."

"So I'm having a party, a little celebration."

"A—a *wedding* party?" Even as Lily spoke, even before Nan's airy chuckle floated down the line, Lily knew she'd got it wrong.

"Not unless one of you is planning to get married."

"'Course we're not," scoffed Lily, though she felt her stupid cheeks grow hot.

"It's for your pop's birthday," Nan explained. "He'll be eighty in September, you know."

Lily hadn't known. Eighty! The sheer weight of it pressed in on her: half a century with another thirty years tacked on—almost five times as long as Lily had lived on earth. Perhaps that explained why he was such an old bigot, so backward in his opinions.

"I want you all to come," urged Nan. "Lonnie especially."

"Lonnie? Nan, you know Pop's not speaking to Lonnie. You know he's written him off. He said so. He said—" Lily deepened her voice, "—'He's no grandson of mine!'"

"He didn't mean it, dear."

"Yes, he did! And what about that ax?"

There was a small pained silence on the line before Nan spoke again. "Pure bluff, dear. You know your pop's all talk. But I'll get rid of that ax if it bothers you."

"It bothers me if Pop's got hold of it."

Nan's voice went stern again. "Your grandpa's not a maniac, Lily."

Now Lily was silent, picturing her grandfather: his short square body, his red face, and little piggy black eyes. The way he could be really, really nice and then, quite suddenly, go crazy. She thought it quite possible he was some kind of maniac.

"Lily?"

"Yes?"

"Could you do something for me? Could you go around to that place where Lonnie lives and tell him about the party? So I can be sure he gets the message? We really want him to come to the celebration."

Celebration! More like a massacre if Pop and Lonnie got together, thought Lily. And who was "we"? Not Nan and Pop, for sure. More like Nan and her imaginary companion.

"Could you?" pleaded Nan.

"Oh, all right," sighed Lily.

"Oh Lily, thank you! You're a treasure, dear." For some reason this compliment made Lily feel uncomfortable. "No, I'm not."

"Don't be silly, dear. Of course you are. Now, is Marigold at home?"

"She's still at work."

"At work?" Nan's voice became incredulous. "But it's *dark* outside!"

And now Lily pictured her grandmother standing by the phone in her kitchen, turning her small face to look out the window at the garden and the thick black winter night.

"It's winter now, Nan. Gets dark early, and Mum doesn't finish till six or later."

"That's shocking, dear."

What could you say to that? Nan came from a different world. "Mum likes her work, Nan. Really."

"You think I'm a silly old softie, don't you?" said Nan.

"No, no, of course I don't," said Lily, startled, as she always was, when her nan said something sharp.

"Bit of a loony, eh?"

"No!"

"Oh, you *do*. But I don't mind. Now tell me, what are the two of you having for dinner?"

"Dunno." Lily ran a hand through her tousled hair. "I haven't really thought about it yet."

"That's the worst part, isn't it, thinking of what to cook?

Now here's an idea for you, Lily—"

"What?"

The airy chuckle came again. "Why don't you get Meals on Wheels?"

12 VANISHING DREAMS

Lily and her mum were watching a movie on television. Or rather, they appeared to be watching, sitting side by side on the sofa, their eyes fixed on the screen. But if anyone had asked them who that woman in the big hat was or what the man rifling through the desk drawers was searching for, they wouldn't have been able to reply.

Their minds were elsewhere. Lily was thinking dreamily of Daniel Steadman and then angrily deciding how humiliating it was to be dreaming of him. She felt she was becoming the kind of person she really didn't want to be. Yesterday at school she'd walked past the senior common room five whole times in the hope that she'd catch a glimpse of him: four times the door had been closed; on the fifth it was open, but he'd been standing at the window with his back to her. She hadn't been able to see his face, and he hadn't even known she was there.

Lily squirmed on the sofa. Fancy spending a whole lunchtime walking past the senior common room! It was pathetic! She'd have been better off in the library doing her homework or writing out her grocery list or sneaking out to the hardware store to buy that washer for the kitchen faucet.

Marigold was fretting about old Mrs.. Nightingale, whose children still hadn't found anyone definite to care for their mother while they went on their second honeymoon. Marigold felt guilty every time she saw them in the dayroom, waiting for their mother to finish her game of solitaire; she knew that if it hadn't been for her promise to Lily, she could have solved their problem quite easily. It was only three days, after all. Three little days. Perhaps Lily would make an exception for such a short time? And then Marigold remembered old Mrs. Edwards's stay with them—which had also been for three days—how the old lady had mistaken Lily for her mother and cried every morning when Lily went off to school Then there was Mr. Roberts—two days—who'd kept going through their drawers and cupboards. Lily had come home to find him out in the garden wearing her yellow dungarees.

Mrs. Nightingale wasn't in the least like them: she didn't wander, either with her feet or in her mind. She played her games of solitaire and read her books, and she wouldn't, Marigold knew, be seen dead in Lily's yellow dungarees. And they had Lonnie's room vacant now ...

"Lily?"

"Yeah?" Lily turned, and Marigold saw she was wearing that furious expression that always reminded Marigold of Pop. Her eyes were black and glittering, and her cheeks had turned bright red. She looked very, very angry. Marigold drew back nervously. What could be the matter? A bad mood? Something wrong at school? Marigold didn't like to ask, and it definitely wasn't the time to suggest a visit from Mrs. Nightingale; she'd simply be letting herself in for a lecture on being unprofessional. Instead she jabbed a finger at the screen. "Um, I just wondered ... have you worked out who that woman in the big hat is?"

"No."

Marigold sighed and began to fret about another problem: the party Mum was having for Pop's eightieth and her insistence that Lonnie should be there. And how could that be, when Pop and Lonnie weren't speaking and any time you mentioned Lonnie's name, Pop would roar, "He's no grandson of mine!"? And Lonnie was so difficult to get hold of, too—Marigold had phoned him several times these last few weeks, and never once had he been at home. At least that was preferable to having him lying in bed all day doing nothing, getting older, except why was he out all the time? How long was it since she'd actually spoken to Lonnie? Heard his voice?

"Lily?"

"Huh?"

"How long is it since Lonnie called?"

"Dunno." She added, disconcertingly, "Ages, isn't it?"

"How long is ages?"

"Three weeks? Four? No, hang on; it was that time he wanted you to send his Army Surplus jacket over."

"But that was at the end of *June*. And now it's August!"

"So?" Lily glared at the screen. "He's okay, Mum. Or do you think his landlady's bumped him off and buried him underneath the floorboards?"

"Of course I don't!" Why couldn't Lily be more sympathetic? It was awful never knowing how Lonnie was getting on or what kind of place he was living in—this gentlemen's boarding house at 5 Firth Street, Toongabbie. Marigold had occasionally been tempted to sneak over there and take a look, only—well, you had your pride, didn't you? She wouldn't spy. She wouldn't stoop so low. Old Mr. Parker at the day-care center had once lived in Toongabbie, and last Tuesday Marigold had asked him if he knew Firth Street. "Never heard of it!" he'd said. Of course, the Toongabbie Mr. Parker had known was sixty years ago. Still, it had given Marigold the most uneasy feeling, as if the place where Lonnie had told them he lived wasn't really there.

And then there were the vanishing dreams. "I had another vanishing dream last night," she said to Lily when the next commercial flashed upon the screen.

"Right!" said Lily, who'd dreamed Tracy Gilman was going out with Daniel Steadman. She'd woken feeling furious, almost on the verge of tears, and it hadn't helped when Tracy had said to her at the end of second period, "You look like you've been crying!"

"Allergy," Lily had said curtly, because she certainly didn't feel like telling Tracy how she'd squirted the can of Easi-Clean the wrong way round.

"I dreamed I got a parcel in the mail," her mum was babbling. "A big brown parcel, like the ones Nan sends sweaters in, and I knew Lonnie was inside. It said so on the label. It said: Fragile. Lonnie inside."

"Fragile!" scoffed Lily.

"Only he wasn't inside. There were layers and layers of paper, and then—nothing."

"Sounds like Lon."

"Lily!"

"Mum, you've got to stop worrying about him. He's a big boy now, you know; he's twenty-two! He can look after himself."

"I know," said Marigold. "It's just that, when you're a mother—"

"Your brain softens."

"Not at all," said Marigold coldly. "But you do always tend to think the worst. You lie awake, and you—"

Lily didn't want to hear about lying awake. She thought

being a mother must be like having an eternal crush. "If it makes you feel better, I'm going to Lon's place tomorrow," she said.

"Where? To the boarding house?"

"Yeah."

"But you know Lonnie doesn't want us to go there. He—he said he needed space."

"He's had space," said Lily, who felt she had no space at all, because having a crush was like a prison. It was like solitary confinement. "And I'm not going there to spy, Mum—" she saw her mother flinch, "—I'm going because Nan asked me. She wants to be sure Lon knows about Pop's party."

"Oh, that wretched party," Marigold said, sighing.

Lily understood her mother's tone. Parties in their family always seemed to end in fights. Or even start with them, like this one would if Lonnie came along and Pop was still disgusted with him. "I'm going there before school, really early," she told her mother, "so I'll be sure to catch him in, and I'll try and get him to make up with Pop."

"Oh, Lily, do you think you can?"

"No," said Lily. "But I'll have a go at it."

"Your nan's so looking forward to this party. And so is Sef."

Lily stared at her mother, appalled. "Mum, do you *believe* in Sef? Do you think she's *real?*"

Marigold's face turned pink. "No, of course not! It's just, I'm so used to her, you see."

Used to her. What did that mean? Mum was getting weird. Lily sighed and turned back to the movie, but she couldn't get the hang of the story, and this time it wasn't because she was daydreaming about Daniel Steadman. It was because she could sense Mum staring at her.

Lily swiveled around. "What are you looking at?"

"Just you," said Marigold tenderly. "I don't know what I'd do without you, Lily."

Lily flushed, pleased and embarrassed. "You'd fill the house with lame ducks, Mum," she said gruffly. "That's what you'd do. And in the end—"

"In the end?"

"You'd probably marry one of them."

"Of course I wouldn't. Though—" Marigold smiled slyly at her daughter,"—I have had offers."

"*Who?*"

"Old Captain Cuthbert asked me to set up ship with him last week."

"Mum, he's *crazy.*" An awful thought struck Lily. "You didn't say yes, did you?"

"Of course not. Though I was tempted, mind you."

"You're joking, aren't you, Mum? Aren't you?"

Marigold tweaked a lock of Lily's hair. "'Course I am."

They settled back down to the movie, and now Lily *was* daydreaming. She was imagining Danny Steadman saying to her, "I don't know what I'd do without you, Lily."

"Do you know what they're all looking for?" asked her mother suddenly, nodding toward the vague figures on the screen.

"Search me."

Marigold giggled, and then Lily began to giggle, too, and a small mouse, emerging unnoticed from a hole at the bottom of the skirting board, looked at them in surprise.

13 THE BOARDING HOUSE FOR GENTLEMEN

Why did he have to live all the way out here? Lily was fuming as she made her way along the early morning streets of Toongabbie, an icy wind whipping at the hem of her school skirt, the tip of her frozen nose, and the sodden corkscrews of her hair. Why couldn't he live in the kind of place where other students lived: a hall of residence, a hostel, a shared house somewhere near the university? Why live in a boarding house? Why live way out here? She'd had to get up at six and take two trains, and after she'd seen Lonnie and safely delivered Nan's message, she'd have to take two trains back again to school.

Lonnie would have his reasons, of course, but they wouldn't be the kind of reasons anyone else would choose. In her family, people seemed to make important changes in their lives for weird reasons, without exactly meaning to. Look how she'd become a sort of airhead, obsessed with Daniel Steadman, simply because she'd grown tired of being the sensible one in the family. And Mum had once confessed to her that she'd married their father because she'd loved his coat.

"Coat?" Lily had echoed, thinking—as any normal person would—that she'd misheard.

Only she hadn't. "He had this lovely coat his great-aunt had given him for his twenty-first birthday: she'd bought it in Peru. Oh, Lily, it had the most beautiful colors, colors I'd never seen before. I was quite young, remember."

"Yeah, but—"

"And the most wonderful texture!" her mother had gone on dreamily. "A mixture of rose petals and the softest sort of fur."

"You married someone because you liked his *coat?*"

"Oh no, of course not. But the coat was part of it, part of *everything.*" Her mother had sighed then, the sort of sigh a very old lady might give while recalling childhood summers.

Lily skirted a row of icy puddles beside a construction site and then stopped to consult the map she'd made from Mum's street directory. The wind was vicious, stinging at her cheeks and flapping the piece of paper in her hand: Firth Street was the next left, then the third right. Lily walked on. Lonnie had probably moved out here because he fancied living in a gentlemen's boarding house, and 5 Firth Street was the only one left in Australia. Or—Toongabbie was on the rail line to the mountains— perhaps, on the day Pop had quarreled with him, Lonnie's train had passed this place at the very second he'd decided to leave home; and Lonnie might have looked out through the window and decided, "I'll live here!"

Perhaps he just liked the name, Toongabbie.

Freakish, thought Lily. That was the word that best described their family. Not freaks, exactly, but getting there. They were a family that somehow didn't fit—at least not into the orderly suburb where they lived, a neighborhood in which any human problem was tidied out of sight, clipped, wrenched out, composted, so that it seemed, like the vanished weeds in gardens, that it had never ever been there. Sometimes Lily felt there was an aura about her, a scent of danger as well as cooking smells that hung about her hair and skin and clothes, so that people, without knowing they were doing it, backed off from her.

People like Daniel Steadman. He probably *knew* about her family. Last week, in the courtyard of the library, Lily had seen Tracy Gilman deep in conversation with Daniel. Tracy lived in Lily's street, just four doors down, in a perfect house with windows that shone, paintwork that was glossy and whole, and lawns that were like brilliant green velvet even in the middle of a drought. Lily hadn't been able to hear what they were saying, and it might have had nothing to do with her (having a crush on someone seemed to make you paranoid), but she couldn't help thinking Tracy *could* be telling him about that afternoon she'd walked home with Lily, and old Mr. Roberts, one of mum's lame ducks, had been in their front garden wearing Lily's yellow dungarees.

And you didn't have to be paranoid to realize that there were people at school who remembered Lonnie, even though it was four whole years since he'd been there. Teachers would stop Lily in the corridor and ask her, "How's your brother doing, dear?" and she could see a kind of avid goggle in their eyes that meant they were expecting some disaster story. Okay, Lily herself felt pretty fed up with Lonnie sometimes, but those goggle-eyed teachers made her angry because when you really got down to it, there wasn't anything *seriously* wrong with Lonnie—it was simply that he could never seem to stick to anything. And hadn't she been like that when she was little? First she'd tried ballet and given it up, then Brownies; then there was the saxophone—though of course, she'd been little then ...

Loser, fumed Lily. Why should he go away and leave her there to be the sensible one of the family? No wonder she'd gone funny about Daniel, spending her lunchtimes walking past the senior common room.

Lily skipped another icy puddle and a bunch of slimy leaves. Where on earth was Firth Street? She'd been walking down this road for ages, and Firth Street never came. Perhaps that was how it was with Lonnie, she thought. He was like a person walking down a long, long road waiting for the corner, the right corner, that would lead into the street where he needed to be. *Loser!* She was going to tell him off when she got there. She really, truly, was.

"Gone?" echoed Lily, gazing fearfully into the fierce blue eyes of Lonnie's landlady. Although it had taken her such a long time to find the boarding house, it was still only seven forty-five, and her brother had never gotten up that early, even when he'd been at school. Poor Mum had had to call and call …

A sudden panic gripped her, a panic she recognized as being straight out of her mother's vanishing dreams. "Do you mean he's *left*?" she whispered. "Gone to live somewhere else?"

Disappeared. Gone somewhere else, and then somewhere else, so they'd never ever find him again—Lily suddenly glimpsed how simple something unimaginable might be.

The landlady smiled at her. "Of course not, dear. He's just gone to an early tutorial at the university."

"But he never goes to early tutorials," exclaimed Lily, the words springing to her lips before she had time to think. She flushed with embarrassment, and Mrs. Rasmussen smiled again. "I think you'll find he does so now," she said, and then Lily was smiling, too, because Lonnie was still doing his course and Mum was going to be thrilled about that, and Nan would be thrilled too, and even Pop might put away his stupid ax, and Nan could have her party without actual

warfare, as if she lived in the kind of family where such celebrations passed off without a hitch. "Can I leave a message?"
she asked.

"Of course you can." Mrs. Rasmussen waited to hear what
Lily would say.

"Um, I meant, would it be all right if I wrote him a note and
left it in his room?" She wasn't spying, Lily told herself, only
there was no way she was leaving this place without seeing
what Lonnie's room was like.

For Mum's sake, anyway. Mum would want to know every
detail. "It—it's private," she said.

"Ah, privacy," said Mrs. Rasmussen softly.

"I didn't mean, um—"

"I was young once, too." The landlady smiled and, taking
a key from the ring at her waist, handed it to Lily. "Room
number seven, second floor."

Up the narrow stairway, down a gloomy hall. Lily turned
the key in her brother's door and took a deep breath before
she pushed it open. But there was nothing for Mum to worry
about here. The room was almost an exact replica of the one
Lonnie had left behind: the single bed beneath the window,
duvet tumbled to the floor, pizza boxes and take-out cartons,
old newspapers, a snowdrift of clothes by the door. Only the
desk looked different: the single clear surface in the cluttered
room, books neatly stacked on one side, notes and folders on
the other, an essay with red comments scrawled angrily inside
the margins. Lily took a step toward it and then stopped short.
No! She wouldn't look at it—Lonnie, she realized suddenly,
would never spy on her. Lonnie let people be; it was one of
his good points. He hardly ever criticized.

Lily sat down on the edge of the bed, twitched off her

backpack, fumbled inside it, tore a sheet from her notepad, and scribbled: *Nan's party: you have to come. And for Nan's sake, please, please make up with Pop!*

As she touched his pillow to place the note on it, a small square of paper escaped from beneath it and fluttered to the floor. Lily bent and picked it up. She didn't mean to read it, did she? Only you couldn't help but see how there was only one word on that sheet, a single name, written over and over again. "Clara," whispered Lily, and she didn't have a clue why the sound of that name and the idea that Lonnie had a girlfriend should make her so happy and then, almost at once, so sad.

Sad? No, be honest, Lily told herself sternly, standing in the center of the little room and gulping in a breath of freezing air. She was envious. Envious of Clara, or of any girl who had someone who would like her so much he would write her name like that, over and over and over.

14 LONNIE RECLAIMS THE MORNING

Lonnie had forgotten early mornings; he'd forgotten the ice on winter puddles, the smoke of his breath on the air. He'd forgotten how sounds were clearer: the smart clack of his footsteps on the pavement, dogs barking, voices calling, the distant slam of a door.

"Do they still have that early morning tutorial in Anglo-Saxon in First Year?" Clara had asked him a few days ago. "You know, the one at nine on Thursday?"

There *was* such a tutorial. Lonnie had seen it on his time-table and stared at it with incredulity: what did they mean by holding a class at such a criminal hour? Didn't they have any imagination? Didn't they know that students had actual lives? After some consideration, Lonnie had decided not to go. With his part-time stacking job and all his reading and assignments, Lonnie rarely got to bed before twelve. Reaching the university by nine meant he'd have to get up before seven; he'd be worn out for the rest of the day. Wasted. He wouldn't be able to take in anything, and what was the use of that? Besides, there was this kid in Second Year who'd promised to lend him his notes—

"Because," Clara had continued, "I've got a nine o'clock on Thursdays, too, so I thought we could meet in the Union, at eight thirty, and have breakfast together."

Going out with Clara seemed to put a whole new gloss on things. Suddenly a nine o'clock tute didn't seem quite so criminal. Even eight thirty was … fine. Breakfast with Clara! It was the word "together" that undid him, though. Clara said it so naturally, as if the pair of them had always been … well, together.

"Together!" he chanted every Thursday morning in Mrs. Rasmussen's bathroom, while he showered, shaved, and cleaned his teeth. "Together, together, together!" It banished the dark at the windows, the icy touch of the linoleum, the cold intimidation of that sign up on the wall: "Please leave this bathroom as you find it."

"Together" made the dark walk down to the station seemed exhilarating, transformed the scowling early-morning workers on the platform into human beings—almost, though not quite, made you think that even Anglo-Saxon grammar might hold charms.

When had he last seen early morning? wondered Lonnie, resting his elbow on the dusty windowsill of the city-bound train and watching the suburbs roll by. Back at school, it must have been—the Year Eleven camp, and that was five whole years ago! Five years that had trickled away like a bucket of water into sand.

On the track beside him, another train drew level, and for a second Lonnie thought he glimpsed his sister's face. It couldn't be Lil, of course; at this time of the morning she would still be at home washing the breakfast dishes, checking the fridge to see there was something for dinner, frowning at the laundry basket, packing her homework into her bag. Something unexpected stirred in Lonnie then, something guilty and surprised. Perhaps he should have helped her more when he'd been at home—he was hopeless at housework and stuff, though. He'd only have gotten in her way, made things worse. Lily had always been the sensible one in the family, the efficient one, the early riser; and how surprised she'd be if she knew he was up and about so early, heading off to breakfast with his girlfriend, then on to a tute at nine. Nine!

How glorious the city looked outside the windows, the sun on the rooftops, rimming them with gold, the small pink clouds melting into the blue. "Reclaim the morning!" cried Lonnie, punching his fist in the air. People turned to stare at him. Lonnie didn't mind at all. Everyone seemed beautiful today.

"I think he's got a girlfriend," Lily told her mother. "There was a little sheet of paper with a name written over and over. Clara, it was."

Marigold swung around from the fridge where she was putting away the shopping. "Oh, I'm so glad!" she said, and Lily felt almost resentful. All Mum could think of was Lonnie—if Lily ever got to tell Mum she had a boyfriend, Mum's face wouldn't glow like that, as if angels were descending.

"I'm not sure, of course," she went on. "It might simply be some girl he's got a crush on, who doesn't even know he's there." An image of Daniel flashed into Lily's mind. She shook her head and he vanished. Good! All you needed was willpower.

By evening the news had traveled to the hills. "Stan!" May called through the kitchen window. Stan was out in back mowing again. "Stan! Guess what!"

Stan turned off the mower. "Yeah?"

"Lonnie's got a girlfriend! Her name's Clara!"

So the little no-hoper had a girlfriend, did he? So what!

Stan started the mower up again.

May turned from the window. "Cranky old bugger, isn't he?" she said to her friend Sef.

15 HOSPITALITY

Jessaline O'Harris lay in bed reading. It was ten o'clock, and she was skipping her lecture in Old Norse. Jessaline had never skipped a lecture before, and it gave her a wild, delicious feeling that was almost criminal. She was sure she must look different, too.

Jessaline jumped out of bed, removed her glasses, and peered at her face in the mirror over the sink. There was a dangerous glint in her eye that hadn't been there before, and surely her chin had changed its shape? Become more pointed and determined? Had it? Or was she imagining things? Jessaline twisted her head this way and that, trying to make up her mind. Then she put on her glasses and skipped out into the hall. "Clara!" she called, knocking on Clara's door. "Clara!"

No one answered, and then Jessaline remembered that Clara had an early tute at nine o'clock on Thursdays, so she went back to bed, took up her book, and began reading again.

Bavarian Crème Perfect Love: Mix two cups sugar and eight yolks of egg until lemon-colored. "Lemon-colored," whispered Jessaline, enraptured. *Slowly add two cups hot milk in which six cloves have been heated …*

A few hours later Jessaline crossed the highway and entered the place her parents and other snobby people from the university called the Hinterland: the place where the schools of Hospitality, Cosmetic Science, Phys Ed, and other nonacademic disciplines had their homes. Here, even the landscape was different. Instead of well-tended gardens and lawns and courtyards, Jessaline passed through a simple strip of bushland, emerging suddenly onto a netball court.

"Watch out!"

"Look where you're going!"

Jessaline ducked and weaved between the players. "I'm sorry, I didn't mean—I didn't know—" she murmured, but they paid her no attention. In the Hinterland, it seemed, people didn't apologize. Jessaline crossed a small paddock of bristly unmown grass and headed determinedly toward a low red brick building, which squatted solid and foursquare by a narrow roadway ... She stumbled on the steps. Her eyes were astigmatic: she could see out of each of them quite clearly, but it was hard to get them working together. *Captain Cutlass School of Hospitality*, she read on the gray glass doors. Jessaline frowned. It seemed an odd name for a university department, even in the Hinterland—and wasn't Captain Cutlass a character from a children's picture book?

"Can I help you?"

The girl at reception looked terribly young to Jessaline. Could this be a sign that she herself was getting old? Perhaps she'd got here just in time—she'd be twenty in December, after all. Twenty! "I'm thinking of getting a changeover," she told the girl shyly.

"Changeover?" The girl stared at Jessaline's pebbly glasses and her flumpy, mouse-brown hair. "You're in the wrong place then. This is Hospitality." She pointed through the window. "Cosmetic Science is over there."

"Changeover, not makeover," said Jessaline coldly. "I'm thinking of changing *courses*. Changing to Hospitality."

The girl leaned her chin on one hand. "From what?" she asked, and Jessaline could see, from the computer closed beside her and the copy of *Bestie* brazenly open at page 47 (*Is Your Boss a Psychopath?*) that the question sprang from nothing more than idle curiosity.

"Linguistics."

"What's that?"

Jessaline smiled at her. She was beginning to like this girl. There was no nonsense about her—she was as solid and four-square as the building that sheltered her.

"The study of languages," she said, and the girl said, "Aargh. Rather you than me."

"Precisely," replied Jessaline. "I'm not suited. That's why I want to change. I want to do Hospitality. I want to cook, *really* cook, I want to work in a famous restaurant, and perhaps, one day, to have—"

"Okay, okay." The girl waved an elegant white hand. Her nails were painted a deep and thrilling blue. "I get the message."

"So I wanted to know if I could change over next semester."

"Next semester? I think you can, but—"

"But what?"

"But you'll have to go over *there*." The girl flapped her hand toward another window, one that gave a clear view of the highway and beyond it the tall graceful buildings of the "proper" university. "To Admin. They'll tell you what to do, give you all—" she wrinkled her small nose in distaste, "—the forms and stuff."

"Thank you," said Jessaline, and she turned to go.

"Look forward to seeing ya!"

"What?" Jessaline spun around.

The girl was smiling at her. "Look forward to seeing ya. You know, next year, when you get your course fixed up."

"Oh, yes!" Jessaline's face glowed. They were so friendly over here! The woman in the office at Linguistics never spoke to students if she could avoid it. Emboldened, Jessaline pointed to the sign upon the door. "Why's it called Captain Cutlass School of Hospitality?"

"Captain Cutlass?"

"On the door there."

"It's not Captain Cutlass. You must need new glasses."

"Oh, I do. I can't see the edges on things."

The girl nodded. "Get contacts, then. Those glasses don't suit you—they wouldn't suit anyone."

"I know." Jessaline pointed to the door again. "So what does it say?"

"It's Cathleen Cuthbert. Cathleen Cuthbert School of Hospitality."

"Cathleen Cuthbert?"

"Someone's wife, I guess." The girl shook her head sadly. "Fancy dying and having a cookery school called after you."

"Better than a school of linguistics," said Jessaline.

They grinned at each other. "Bye," said Jessaline.

"See ya," said the girl.

As she walked down the steps Jessaline noticed that the sky above her was a deep translucent blue. And the air in the strip of bushland smelled of eucalyptus and some other fine sharp scent she couldn't identify—it was, quite simply, a truly perfect day. And at two o'clock Jessaline had a lecture on the phonology of Old English. She tossed her head and gave a little skip. Catch her going there! Instead she went to Mrs. Murphy's flat in the basement of Mercer Hall.

"It's only me," she said when Mrs. Murphy opened the door. A delicious smell of baking wafted out into the hall.

"*Only* you!" cried Mrs. Murphy, beaming. "*Only* the person I most love to see!"

Jessaline stepped inside.

16 BENEATH THE PEPPER TREES

Beneath the pepper trees, the Year Ten girls were talking about asking boys out: walking up to a boy you fancied and asking him if he'd like to go to a movie with you, or a concert, or a party, or even a simple coffee at the mall. Men and women were equals, weren't they? So why not? Those days were gone when a girl had to hang about waiting to be asked. Or were they?

Because, in practice, asking a boy out, at least in a place like Flinders High, could actually be quite difficult. For a start, it was hard to get a boy alone. Boys were mostly with other boys, and who'd want to ask someone you fancied with a whole bunch of his friends looking on? Hooting and whistling perhaps, so the boy you fancied might say no even if he really wanted to say yes.

"You could go to his house if you wanted to get him alone," suggested Molly Random, who, while she wasn't exactly slow, was sort of … lagging, everyone agreed. Nice, but definitely lagging.

"His house?" snapped Lara Reid. "And then his mum opens the door, and she grills you about who you are and what's your business, and then when the boy comes out, *if* she lets him, he's all red and useless, and he can't wait for you to get right out of there."

There was an angry edge to Lara's voice so that all the other girls guessed she'd had an experience of that kind herself, which was why she knew all about it, and they wondered who the boy had been and what exactly his mum had said to Lara.

"It's best if you know him," said Maisie Blair. "Like, if you're in his media class, and you're doing a joint assignment, then it would be sort of natural to ask him if he wants to go to a movie."

"But then he'd be in your *Year!*" cried Lara, and there were sounds of disgust from almost all the girls. Who wanted to go out with a boy in your Year? A boy you'd known since primary school, and possibly even kindergarten? Who'd had disgusting habits when he was a little kid, even if he'd curbed them now.

"Remember how Cameron Webb used to eat snails in Year Two?" asked Molly Random. "Those big snails from Mrs. Archer's fish tank?"

"Moll!"

"Well, he did!"

Boys in Year Ten simply weren't desirable. How could they ever be?

They all favored older boys, the ones in Year Twelve and Year Eleven, or boys who'd left school and were working or studying at the university.

"You've simply got to get to know them first," blurted Lizzie Banks suddenly. "Or get them to notice you at least."

No one replied to this. Lizzie was notorious for her crush on Simon Leslie, the vice-captain of the school. For the past three months, Lizzie had jogged past his front fence every evening, and sometimes mornings too. She was hoping Simon would see her and come out. So far he never had. Or, as Tracy Gilman had unkindly suggested, he'd spotted her and stayed inside. "Honest, Liz," said Tracy now. "You should—"

"What?" Poor Lizzie flushed.

"Give up on him."

"Who's *him?*"

"Oh, come off it. Simon Leslie. Who else?"

"You should try jogging in the park instead," suggested Maisie kindly. "You might meet a really tasty jogger there, and you'd have something in common with him, to start off."

"I don't like joggers," said Lizzie. "They smell sweaty even when they've had a shower and changed into proper clothes."

There was a silence underneath the pepper trees.

"Male joggers, I mean," said Lizzie hastily. "It's the male joggers who smell sweaty."

This was awful, thought Lily. So awful it made you almost wish you weren't a girl. And it sapped your willpower, too, because already she'd started thinking, how could she get Daniel Steadman to notice her?

"I asked a boy out once," said Carol Dewey suddenly.

"You did?"

"Who was he?"

Lily tensed. What if Carol replied, "Daniel Steadman"? Lily could tell from Carol's expression and something slightly halting in her voice that this was going to be a story of male treachery, and she didn't want Daniel Steadman to be that kind of boy. Lily crossed her fingers behind her back, "Please let it not be him," she prayed.

"What Year was he in?" Lara asked.

"Year Twelve."

Lily relaxed. Daniel was in Year Eleven.

"Leo Harmon?" guessed Lara.

"'Course not! As if I'd want to ask him out!"

"Simon Leslie?" said Tracy slyly.

"No!" Carol stole a quick apologetic glance at Lizzie. "Honest, it wasn't!"

"Who, then?"

"Gareth Castle," whispered Carol.

There was an indrawn gasp beneath the pepper trees. Gareth Castle was the glorious captain of the cricket team.

"You asked *Gareth Castle* out?"

"Where to?"

"Just to a movie."

"Gareth Castle's lovely," said Molly, and then she added, scanning Carol's face and sensing something not quite right, "I mean, he *looks* lovely."

"What did he say?"

Carol's voice was flat. "He said, 'Don't want to.'"

There was another gasp, and Carol burst out, "Stuck-up pig! 'I don't want to'—can you imagine? Like a little four-year-old. No, a two-year-old!" She swept her lunch box from her lap, scattering crusts and apple cores onto the grass. She sprang to her feet and stood very straight, her fists clenched by her side. "What's wrong with *me?*"

She shouldn't have said that, thought Lily.

Carol Dewey was the most beautiful girl in Year Ten—tall and slender, with a creamy complexion, features that were very nearly perfect, and long wavy corn-silk hair. There was nothing the least bit wrong with her except, now that she'd asked this question, the eyes of almost all the Year Ten girls swept up and down her searching eagerly for some flaw.

"Your ears," said Tracy Gilman.

Carol's hands flew up. "You mean they're too big?"

"No, not big."

Molly shook her head. "Not big," she echoed.

"They stick out, you mean?" Carol's lovely face contorted with a kind of fright.

"No, not that," said Tracy slowly, and Molly echoed her again, "Not that."

"Then what? *What?*"

"It's just that one of them is—only a little bit, mind you, but noticeable all the same—"

"*What? Which one?*"

"The left one," said Tracy helpfully. "It's bigger than the other."

"Oh!" Carol turned from them and fled across the oval, her hands clasped over her ears.

Headed for the mirrors in the washroom, Lily guessed. "Her ears are the same size," she said to Tracy, and Molly Random said, "They are. *Exactly* the same size."

"That wasn't fair, Trace," said Lizzie.

"It was mean," said Molly.

"She asked, didn't she? She asked if there was anything wrong with her."

"Only so we'd say there wasn't."

Tracy shrugged. "It was only a joke," she said. "She'll get over it."

Yes, sometimes Lily really did wish she wasn't a girl. Or at least not one like Tracy Gilman.

17 CLARA'S ROOM

Finished! Clara pressed the Save button on her computer and leaned back in her chair. At once images of Lonnie swam into her mind: his tall, gangly figure loping across the campus toward her, briefcase tucked under his arm. The way he had of tossing his head back—like a startled horse, she thought—to free his forehead of that stray lock of floppy, foolish hair. Clara smiled. Even objects that belonged to him were dear to her: that funny old briefcase for instance, so crumpled and ancient she'd thought it might once have belonged to his dad.

"My dad?" he'd stared at her, quite genuinely surprised. "Why would it be his? I bought it at an Op Shop." He'd stroked the smooth, worn leather. "Only two bucks! Great bargain, eh?"

He didn't really seem to mind the loss of his father when he was little, but Clara minded for him. She'd wake up in the middle of the night and lie there thinking about a very small Lonnie following his mother around the house, trailing after her and wailing, "Mum! Mum, when's Dad coming back?" over and over again.

"Poor Lonnie," Clara would whisper, staring into the dark, and she'd wish—childishly, she knew—that she had some kind of time machine that would transport her back then so that she could take the little boy who'd been Lonnie into her arms and comfort him.

If only *her* dad had run away, thought Clara. If only she could say, as Lonnie did, "I can hardly remember him."

A knock sounded at her door.

"Come in," called Clara, and Jessaline appeared, carrying a tray on which rested a beautiful golden cake with a frosting of snowy powdered sugar.

She laid the tray gently on the coffee table. Then she stood back, skipped a little, and flung her arms out wide. "I've done it!" she exclaimed.

Clara looked down at the cake. "It's wonderful," she said.

"Oh, not that!" said Jessaline dismissively. "I didn't mean the cake. It's just an apple cake Mrs. Murphy and I whipped up this afternoon. What I meant was—" Jessaline clasped her hands together. Behind the thick pebbly glasses her eyes shone like stars. "Clara, I've made a start!"

"A start? How do you mean?"

"In changing courses!"

"You mean, dropping Linguistics for Hospitality?"

"Yes! I went there today, at lunchtime, to the School of Hospitality. And Clara, I felt really at home there the minute I went through the door. Isn't that strange? How I'd feel at home in a place I'd never been?"

"No," said Clara. "You felt like that because you were meant to be there."

"That's what I thought! And then, when I came out, it was such a beautiful afternoon so I skipped my lecture and went straight around to Mrs. Murphy's flat, and we made this cake—Biba's apple cake, it's called—and, and—" quite out of breath, Jessaline sank down on Clara's bed. "Oh, I've never felt so happy!"

"I'll make the tea," said Clara.

"Oh no, let me!" Jessaline sat up and glanced at the computer. "You've been doing brainwork, I can see."

Brainwork. How Jessaline loved that word, and others like it: *veggies*, and *uni*, and *cossie*, words her parents would have hated and been appalled to hear their daughter use.

Clara smiled. "Not much brainwork. You stay there." She jumped up from her chair, took the electric kettle from its shelf, and turned on the faucet above the tiny sink.

"I saw you with that boy again today," said Jessaline.

"What boy?"

"*You* know! The one I saw you with last Monday—that dreamy-looking fair-haired boy. And the Friday before that, and the Wednesday before that, and—*you* know," she said teasingly.

"Oh, that one," said Clara, trying to sound casual. "He's just a friend." She felt the color rising warmly to her face and turned her head a little, hoping Jessaline wouldn't see.

Jessaline did. "You're *blushing!*"

"No, I'm not. It's just this room. It's so hot!" Clara switched on the kettle and crossed to the window, sliding the glass aside. Behind her, she heard Jessaline say softly, "You looked really good together. You know how people look when they're somehow … right for each other or … or something."

"He's just someone from my English tute, that's all."

"Sorry. You don't want to talk about him."

"It's not that." Clara swung around. "There's nothing *to* talk about. Honest."

"Okay, I'll shut up. Shouldn't be sticking my nose in, anyway. Promise me one thing, though."

"What?"

"When you get married—"

"Jessaline!" Clara should have felt cross. Instead, she giggled like a Year Seven, and Jessaline giggled too. "When you get married, bags I make the wedding cake."

After Jessaline had gone, Clara stayed at the window and looked down on the ocean of city lights. Lonnie's light was far out in the smoky golden haze where the edge of the city rolled on to the darkness of the hills.

Was he thinking of her?

Yes, he was, she sensed it. At this very moment he would be gazing from his window on the first floor of Mrs. Rasmussen's Boarding House for Gentlemen, winging his thoughts in the direction of Mercer Hall. Abruptly, Clara had an image of her mother's face. She heard her saying, "On clear days, Clara, I can actually see your hall from our front porch. I look for it every morning when I go out to fetch the paper and I say to your dad: 'You can see Clara's place today.'"

Mum wanted to see this room. Clara knew it, even though her mother hadn't actually asked. She could read it in her face on those occasions when they had coffee together in town. Mum wanted to see her daughter's private perfect place; she wanted to sit in Clara's chair and drink from Clara's mug, like Goldilocks in *The Three Bears*. And though she loved her mother dearly, Clara wasn't letting her—not yet. It was too soon, too short a time since she'd left home.

Her gaze swiveled eastward to the suburb where her parents lived. She glanced at her watch: 10:35; she knew what they'd be doing, all right. The same thing they did every night: sitting on the sofa watching *Lateline*, poor Mum struggling to make conversation, Dad sitting silent, listening to her try. "Oh Mum," whispered Clara, pressing her forehead against the cold glass of the window, "Mum!" and then with a single savage tug she pulled the curtains across and shut the city out of view.

18 ROSE MAKES A STAND

Clara was wrong. Her mother wasn't watching *Lateline* on the sofa with Clara's dad. She had been for the first ten minutes, but when she'd ventured a comment on the program and Charlie hadn't answered, Rose had said, "Good night!" sharply and left him sitting there. She hadn't even asked if he wanted a cup of tea; she'd marched upstairs to the bathroom, filled the tub to brimming, and poured in half a bottle of the juniper bath oil Clara had given her for Christmas. She'd been saving it ... for what? For tonight, it seemed.

She had never before walked away from Charlie when he'd been sulking. Clara's mum was one of those mild, quiet people who dreaded arguments, who liked to keep the peace, and she wasn't sure why, this evening, she'd finally made a stand, unless it had something to do with the young woman who'd read the 10:30 news tonight, how she'd reminded Rose of Clara, a certain expression Clara had sometimes, her eyes looking out at you sternly from beneath her glossy fringe of hair.

Clara had hated the way her father sometimes wouldn't answer when her mother spoke to him. "Mum!" she would say, quite bossily, to Rose. "Mum, how can you put up with that?"

"It's nothing, darling," Rose would always reply. "Your father's simply tired."

"Tired? Rude, more like."

"Darling, you know he gets tired from work."

"So do *you*."

"I only work four days a week."

"And on the fifth you're running around shopping and washing and doing housework—and what about the food? What about the way he complains about everything you make? You're such a good cook, Mum, and yet everything you make, it's —" Clara contorted her features into her father's sulky scowl, "—'What's this?'" she growled. "'What's this stuff, Rose? Are you trying to poison me?'"

Rose giggled.

"It's no laughing matter, Mum," said Clara angrily.

"Your dad had a very sad childhood, Clara. His parents never really understood him. They were old."

Clara wrinkled her nose, and Rose had no trouble guessing what she was thinking. Old? Weren't all parents old? Wasn't that the defining feature of a parent? "He was a late child," she told her daughter. "His mother was forty-five when he was born, and his dad was well into his fifties. They were more like grandparents, really. It was sad. Do you know they actually had him wearing a suit when he was only three?"

Clara shook her head. "Mum, having ancient parents is simply no excuse—"

"It makes you into a certain kind of person, darling."

"A person who acts like a pig, who takes his miseries out on other people—" Clara paused for breath and then said, "Mum, what about *you*?"

"Me?"

"Yes, *you*. You're the one who had bad things happen in your childhood. Your parents died when you were seventeen, you were the one left all alone, you—"

Rose flinched as she always did when her sad history was mentioned. "I know," she said quickly, wanting this subject of her parents to pass. "But—"

"But, but, but!" cried Clara, her voice rising to a shout. "Mum, why do you always make excuses for him? He's just a rude old grouch!" She marched from the kitchen, where so many of their quarrels seemed to take place, and then stopping suddenly in the doorway, swung around on Rose. "You could leave," she said.

At first Rose didn't realize what her daughter meant. She thought Clara was talking about her job at the library, which Rose enjoyed. She loved books. She liked the patrons and matching one to the other. "You will *love* this!" Rose would greet Mrs. Fitchett, holding out the latest novel from the old lady's favorite author. "It's his best, I think!"

"Leave? But I like my job, Clara."

Clara clicked her tongue impatiently. "Not your job. I meant—" Clara rolled her eyes upward, where both of them could hear the head of the household splashing in the shower.

"Leave your *dad?*"

Clara nodded solemnly. "You've got it, Mum!"

Rose's right hand rose protectively against her heart. The young were so *hard*, she thought. They saw everything so sharply, like—like traffic lights: red meant stop and green meant go and the amber one they had no patience with ...

"You'll never do it, though," said Clara. "Mum, I know what you're hoping for: some kind of miracle, the sort of thing that never happens here on earth, so it's not going to happen here at 46 Harkness Street, Lidcombe. Dad won't change, you know, become the kind of person you like to think he is, deep down inside. It will never happen," she repeated, and then she marched off down the hall.

Two weeks later, after a row with her father about her fourth-year thesis topic, Clara had left home. She lived at the university now and never came home to visit; she phoned Rose at the library, and they met every few weeks at a coffee shop in town.

"What's your room like?" Rose would ask her daughter.

"Oh, just ordinary."

"What kind of furniture?"

"What you'd expect," Clara would answer maddeningly. "A bed, and a desk, and a chair. Little sink in the corner, built-in wardrobe. You know."

"What color are the walls?"

Clara would shrug. "Don't remember. Never noticed, I suppose."

They must be white, decided Rose, and in her mind she pictured a narrow, cold white cell. Bare, too, because Clara hadn't taken anything from home except her books and clothes, and it would have cold, stark, echoing floors. Rose shivered. "Would you like me to make you some curtains?" she'd asked hopefully. "I could come and do the measuring, I wouldn't interrupt your work …"

"I've got curtains, Mum."

Rose had been hoping all these months that Clara would ask her to visit, to see the place where she lived. Clara hadn't, and Rose had been afraid to suggest it. What if Clara said no?

• • •

The water in the bath was growing cold. Rose got out and wrapped herself in a deep green fluffy towel. Then she padded down the hall toward her bedroom, put on her nightdress, and lay down on the bed. She could go there, she thought suddenly. She could go without an invitation and visit Clara's room. Why shouldn't she? Clara was her daughter, her only child, and, except for Charlie, her only relative on earth.

Yes, one day soon, she promised herself, she would go. Just to look, to *see*. On her day off, thought Rose sleepily. Not tomorrow though, tomorrow was too soon. Besides, standing up to Charlie as she'd done tonight deserved a special little celebration of its own. Tomorrow she would take a different trip—back to the suburb where she'd grown up, where she could buy her mother's favorite sweet: a whole lovely box of gulab juman.

Downstairs in the living room, Charlie turned off the television, but he didn't go up to bed. He was too unsettled. What was happening?

Rose had never done that before. Spoken to him in that cool, sharp voice ("Good night!") that sounded like a stranger's, got up, and flounced—yes, flounced, like Clara used to—from the room. She'd even slammed the door. And instead of feeling furious, as he had every right to be, Charlie felt uneasy. Small shivers were running through him. What if Rose decided to—ah no, Rose would never do a thing like that. Charlie got up from the sofa and headed for the stairs.

Though often sulky and silent in speech, Charlie could make a lot of noise about the house; his footsteps clattered on the stairs, doors slammed, faucets were turned on full force. Tonight, though, he walked softly and opened the door of the bedroom gently. He could see from the glow of the hall light that Rose hadn't left him; she was fast asleep beneath the eiderdown. But the relief that surged through him turned suddenly to grievance. Asleep! As if it didn't matter in the least that she'd wounded him.

Charlie turned and walked down the hall to Clara's old room where the door was always closed. He went inside. The emptiness assailed him like a blow. *Grief fills the room up of my absent child,* he remembered his Year Twelve English teacher declaiming, in her small chalky room at the top of the senior stairs. *Lies in his bed, walks up and down with me/ Puts on his pretty looks, repeats his words* … "Poetry consoles," Miss Faringale had told them, and she'd been wrong, because the lines slid through him like a blade.

Charlie crossed to the wardrobe and opened the door. Empty wire hangars jangled inconsolably. Beneath them on the floor lay something pale and crumpled; Charlie bent down and picked it up. It was the soft pink sweater he'd bought last year for Clara's birthday, the sweater she'd worn every day for weeks.

She'd left it here. Charlie folded it carefully and reached up to place it on the shelf. As he did so, another line from Miss Faringale's repertoire pushed into his heart: *How sharper than a serpent's tooth it is/ To have a thankless child.*

That was better, he thought. Now that really did console.

19 BESTIE

Lily switched on her bedside light and took out the copy of *Bestie* she'd brought home. Normally, Lily had no time for magazines like *Bestie*; they were full of scary articles, like *Are you too fat for your cossie? What do they talk about behind your back?* and *I can't stop pulling out my hair!* You didn't have to be particularly sensitive for stuff like that to keep you awake at night, thought Lily, once you started thinking about it. Particularly if you had a crush on someone, because having a crush made you feel vulnerable, and even more vulnerable if the person you had a crush on didn't know you existed. But this afternoon, waiting with her groceries at the supermarket checkout nearest to the newsstand, Lily had caught a glimpse of a tantalizing blurb on *Bestie*'s cover: *"Does he notice you? And how to make him."*

Did he? Did he notice her? Lily had never worked out if that little tremor she felt between herself and Daniel Steadman when they passed each other on the playground or in the corridors was real or simply in her mind. So she'd weakened and bought *Bestie,* hoping it might just … well, tell her something she needed to know.

Now, in the privacy of her own room, she flipped through *Bestie*'s shiny pages:

Makeup, clothes, makeup, clothes, clothes. *What figure type are you?* Makeup, clothes, makeup. *I slept with my bestie's boyf.*

Yuk, thought Lily.

Clothes, makeup, clothes—and at last, *Does he notice you?
And how to make him.*

But the article that had sounded so promising was really
no help at all; it was full of guys talking about what they liked
in a girl, which was:

Beauty

Intelligence

Personality

Sense of humor

Kindness

In short, every gift a good fairy godmother, leaning over
your cradle, could bestow. Every gift you could pretend to—
because that was the gist of the second part of the article:
How to make him: pretend. And who wanted to pretend? Who
wanted to *make* people notice you? Who wanted to make
people do anything? She was out of touch with the world
anyway, thought Lily, that was certain: the "befores" in the
makeover section looked better to her than the "afters."

She flung the magazine aside and set off for the bathroom,
where, if you stepped back far enough, the mirror showed
almost the whole of you, from the middle of your forehead
down to the bottom of your knees.

What figure type are you?

Squat, decided Lily. When you were shortish, as she was,
there was less actual room for any fat to spread, so, really, you
looked plumper than you should, which surely wasn't fair.
She moved up close to the mirror to examine her face: small
straight nose, curved lips, dark eyes, a face that persistently
reminded her of someone she could never seem to identify.
Her eyebrows were too thick, almost bushy. Lily pulled open
a drawer in the bathroom cabinet and took out a pair of twee-

zers; tentatively, she pulled at a stout black hair. She was surprised how much it hurt, and the process took ages—what a waste of time! After ten minutes she tossed the tweezers aside and leaned toward the mirror. Her eyebrows looked no different, except that the skin around them had turned red. A kind of *bulgy* red. Inflamed.

"What's wrong with your eyes?" her mum asked, encountering her in the hall.

"Nothing!" snapped Lily, and then, guilty at her mother's hurt expression, she said in a softer voice, "I was just pluck—" she paused here, sensing that "plucking" would be the wrong word for her mother, who didn't go in for activities of that sort. Her tweezers were for removing splinters and other small emergencies of a noncosmetic nature. "I was just thinning my eyebrows," she amended.

"*Thinning* them?"

You could never win. "Plucking them, then." Lily scowled.

"Why?"

"Because they're too thick. Don't you think they're too thick?"

"No."

"No? Mum, look properly."

Her mother came closer. "They're just definite," she said.

"Definite!" scoffed Lily, but she felt pleased all the same. "Definite" sounded good: clear and reasonable, strong. Lily retreated to the bathroom to look at her definite brows. The skin around them was even pinker now. Lily reached for the Savlon and dabbed it on thickly. Now she bore a distinct resemblance to Santa Claus. She rubbed the cream into her skin, and her eyebrows grew slimy, as if a snail had walked along them. "Never mind," she consoled herself. "Never mind."

When she went back to her room, she found Mum in there, *Bestie* in her hands. She looked up from its pages quite guiltlessly; Mum had been born before the age of privacy. "I thought you didn't like these kind of magazines," she said.

"I don't," snapped Lily. "It's for a project. A report on … on advertising."

"Oh." Her mum flipped the magazine shut, glancing momentarily at the list of contents on the cover. "What's a Boyf?" she asked.

"Boyfriend."

"Ah. *I slept with my beastie's boyf,*" she read slowly. "You mean, this girl was into animal abuse?"

"What?"

"Slept with her beastie's boyf!"

"It's 'bestie,' Mum. Not 'Beastie.'"

"Bestie?"

"Best friend."

"Oh." Her mother began to laugh. "Oh, *dear!*"

"What's so funny?"

"Oh, oh nothing." Her mother stared straight into her daughter's eyes, and Lily suddenly felt that Mum knew all about her crush on Daniel Steadman, knew how she lay awake at nights and thought of him, knew how she couldn't stop herself walking past the senior common room hoping for a glimpse, and even knew how she'd bought this stupid magazine because she'd actually thought it might tell her how to get a boy she liked to notice her.

Mum was frowning now.

"What's the matter?" asked Lily nervously.

"Put some antiseptic on those eyebrows. They look really sore."

"I did."

"Oh, all right." Her mother left the room. Ten minutes later Lily heard her voice from the room next door.

"Lily?"

"Yes?"

"Have you thought of anything we can make for dinner tomorrow night?"

"I'm just getting around to it," Lily said, sighing, and closed her eyes. How old did you have to be, she wondered, before you could get Meals on Wheels?

20 RESTLESS NIGHTS

Clara slept dreamlessly that night, and so did Lonnie, and Jessaline. Marigold took ages to get to sleep because she was still worrying about old Mrs. Nightingale's children finding someone to look after her while they went on their second honeymoon. Mrs. Nightingale herself stayed up very late reading the sonnets of Shakespeare: *Shall I compare thee to a summer's day? / Thou art more lovely and more temperate/ Rough winds do shake the darling buds of May* ...

Lily longed to dream of Daniel Steadman. Lara Reid said that if you wrote a person's name on a slip of paper and placed it beneath your pillow, you would dream of that person. Had Lonnie, too, had that idea? It was rubbish, of course, Year Six girly stuff—*Bestie* stuff, or "Beastie" stuff, as Mum would say. Was it possible that Lonnie had taken to reading *Bestie*? Lily found the very idea of Lonnie sitting up in bed at night reading girls' magazines thoroughly disturbing, because despite all that dropping out, Lonnie was *intelligent*. Lonnie's favorite writer was Emily Brontë. But love, as she'd discovered, even simple crushes, could make you do really funny things, things that weren't like you at all. Look at the way Lizzie Banks jogged past Simon Leslie's place day after day after day in the hope he'd come out and talk to her—Lizzie, who'd always hated any kind of sport!

And look at *her*, look at Lily Samson, writing down Daniel Steadman's name on a page torn from her notebook, though at least she only wrote it once—no need to overdo it, as Lonnie had done. Lily slipped the scrap of paper underneath her pillow and fell asleep at once.

And dreamed of the wrong person, dreamed of Mr. Roberts, the old lame duck Mum had brought home, the one who'd stolen her yellow dungarees. He was wearing them in her dream, and Lily was wearing something soft and silky that she couldn't see properly but somehow knew must be Pop's mum's wedding dress. Bells were ringing. She was getting married to old Mr. Roberts. "No, stop! Stop!" she screamed, and no one heard her. And then she slid into another dream, a dream of a garden adorned with streamers and fairy lights, a long table covered with a white cloth, flowers everywhere: all the details of the party she'd been hearing on the phone from Nan. Boring, she'd thought, and impossible, anyway, with Pop and Lonnie fighting—the sort of happy fantasy that in their family could only end in tears. But there was such a sense of happiness in this dream garden that when Lily woke in the morning, she could still feel it, as if she'd had a vision instead of a dream, and suddenly, inexplicably, she wanted that party almost as much as Nan. The kind of party proper families had: a perfect, happy day ...

Daniel Steadman's throat was itching. Very, very faintly, so that he couldn't tell, floundering through the depths of sleep, whether it really was itching or if he simply dreamed it was. Certainly he *had* been dreaming, the most peculiar dream, where he was standing by the window of the senior common room, talking to his friend Leo Harmon, when he suddenly had this feeling that he should turn around and look toward the open door; only when he did, there was no one there, only the sound of footsteps growing fainter in the corridor. A girl's footsteps ... "Hey! Wait!" he called, trying to run toward the door. His feet wouldn't move. "Hey!" he called again.

"Daniel?"

Daniel blinked. There was light in his room, and his mother was bending over his bed. "Daniel, are you all right? I heard you calling out."

"I had this itchy throat," said Daniel. "Only now it's gone. And then there were these footsteps ..."

"Only a dream," said his mother.

"It didn't seem like one," said Daniel.

Up in the hills Stanley was also having a restless night. He'd been having a lot of them lately, ever since he'd found his mum's old wedding dress down at the back of the shed. He'd go to sleep and then wake up again, trying to remember a dream. Tonight he'd dreamed of that scene in the kitchen seventy years ago, when Mum had shown him and Emmy her wedding dress, and they'd giggled fit to bust.

How come he couldn't remember the color of her eyes? Had they been dark brown like his? Hazel? Blue? Had Mum had blue eyes? Gray? It was such a tiny thing, yet it kept him awake at nights, as if there was something more to it than you'd think, as if it was important to remember and that when he did remember, then something that had gone wrong could be put right.

Bloody nonsense. Why was he thinking like this? Plenty wrong in their family, but what the heck had the color of Mum's eyes to do with anything? He wished he'd never found that wedding dress; like a meal of bad oysters, it seemed to have unsettled him.

Could Mum's eyes have been green? Green didn't ring a bell. Stan shifted restlessly beneath the covers, waking May. "What's wrong?" she asked.

"Do you remember the color of Mum's eyes?"

One of the good things about May was that when you asked her something unexpected, even downright stupid, she never asked you why. Now he waited while she thought this one over carefully, taking a long time before she finally answered, "No, I don't."

You couldn't blame her. Mum had passed away in the first year of their marriage, before Marigold had been born. There was no one left to ask, now that Emmy had gone and he was the only one left. Stan felt he'd gone and lost something important, and lost it carelessly.

"Why don't you go home?" said May, and for a terrifying moment Stan thought she'd finally had enough of him, enough of his tempers and quarrels, and was giving him the chuck.

"Home?" he echoed weakly, because *this* was his home, this house in the mountains, this room, this bed …

"Your mum's place," said May.

"You know it got pulled down. There's only flats—"

"I meant the suburb," said May. "It's still there. The place where you grew up."

"Rent a room there, you mean?"

"Rent a room? What are you talking about?"

"Well, you said, 'Go back home.'"

"Only for a few hours, love. You wouldn't need to rent a room just to walk around the streets for a bit—you know, where you used to go with your mum when you were little. Didn't she use to take you shopping? To the barber's? Things like that?"

"Ah." Relief flooded through him like a warm sweet tide. "It might jog your memory, see?"

So it might, thought Stan.

21 THE OLD PLACE

It was years since Stan had been back to the suburb where he'd grown up, and there'd been changes even then: the bootmaker was gone, and the Ham'n'Beef, where Mum had sent him on summer evenings when it had been too hot to cook, to get sixpence worth of beef and a shilling's worth of ham. The Misses Parr's haberdashery had still been in business, though, and Coco Pedy's Fashions, where Stan had often waited, scarlet and embarrassed, for Mum to come out of the ladies' fitting room.

Now, turning from the station into Good Street, Stan stopped and stood, bewildered. Except for Woolies and the old Royal Hotel, both of them shabby and down at the heel, almost everything was gone. Coco Pedy's was a video shop, the Cash 'n' Carry had become some kind of herbalist's, and on the corner where the Misses Parr had sold their embroidery silks and knitting wools stood the Hong Kong Star Emporium.

Even the people had changed. He stood on the corner for a full ten minutes, and in all that time, apart from a couple of schoolkids, he saw only one Australian face. Saris and veils passed by him, men in funny caps, even a tiny old lady in black pajamas and a big straw hat, the exact replica of a picture in Stan's Grade Two Reader: *Our Oriental Friends*.

Stan's face took on an expression his mother and sister would have recognized: pouched cheeks, pursed lips, a deeply grieved groove between his brows. Stan was in the sulks. Anyone would think he'd caught the Qantas flight to Singapore instead of the 7:30 down to Central! "What did we fight the bloody war for?" he muttered, and at once, almost as if she was standing there beside him, Stan heard Lily's voice.

"Well, you didn't, Pops, did you?"

Okay, so he'd had flat feet, so the army wouldn't take him, or the navy, or the air force. He'd have gone if he could have, though. "Pops!" Lily's voice scolded on inside his head. "You're a racist, Pops!"

"No I'm not. It's just—"

Stan could never find words for the way the world kept changing on him these days so that, standing on the once-familiar corner of his old beat in the city, staring up at the tall buildings whose smooth glossy sides reflected clouds— the din of traffic all around him, the mysterious words of unknown languages, strange music—Stan would feel like some kid in a fairy tale, a kid who'd been asleep inside a mountain for a hundred years and then woken in some foreign, unfamiliar land.

He'd never imagined it could happen here, though, here in the tatty old suburb where he'd been born.

"Pops! Imagine!" Lily's voice again.

"Eh? Imagine what?"

"Imagine if there was a civil war here."

"Here?"

"Yeah. It's not impossible, you know. Australia's not all perfect, like you think."

"Look, I *don't* think."

She never let him finish. "And imagine you were on the losing side and got kicked out—"

"What?"

"And you had nowhere to go except on some tatty old boat to another country, with *nothing*, and then, when you got there, to this other country, people started giving you a bad time, especially the *old* ones. Called you names and—"

"I don't call them names."

"Huh! Look how you're saying 'them.'"

"It wouldn't bother me if they called me names," Stan had said stiffly.

"Oh yes? I bet it would. Pop, people from other countries are human, like us."

"No, they're not."

"What?" Lily's voice had risen dangerously. "Not *human?*"

"No, that's not what I meant," Stan had replied, aggrieved. "You always take me the wrong way, Lil. I didn't mean they weren't human, only that, well ... they're different."

"How do you know? How do you know they're not like us, Pop? Have you ever really met an Asian person? Gotten to know one? Ever in your life? Made a friend?"

He'd got her gist. She thought he was one of those types who wouldn't give a home to refugees, who chucked boat people overboard, locked them up in prisons, kids included.

Stan felt hard done by. Of course he wasn't like that! "Just because I get things wrong sometimes," he began, "use the wrong words, and—"

She mowed him down before he'd hardly started.

"Wrong words! Is that what you call it, Pop?"

"Ms. Politically Correct!"

"Big bigot!"

It was funny, he thought, how he and Lil could row and

row, bawling insults at each other, and yet they never really fell out; he never lost her the way he'd lost Lonnie …

Wait a minute! What was he thinking about? He hadn't *lost* Lonnie—he'd chucked him out. He'd written him off, hadn't he? Lonnie was no loss to him.

Now he was hungry. He always got hungry when he got worked up. Time for a Chiko roll, he thought. Yeah, he really fancied a good old Chiko roll. And with a small sigh of anticipation, Stan set off in search of a decent take-out.

Though Stan hadn't noticed, it was a beautiful day, the kind of day you get occasionally at the end of winter after months of wind and cold and rain. Through the grimy window of her westbound train, Clara's mum could see a sky the color of new satin ribbon, a true and perfect cerulean. The shabby old weatherboards beside the railway seemed to have a shine to them. There were fat green buds on the trees along the nature strips, and freesias and little white daisies coming up through the grass on the embankments. In a few short weeks it would be spring.

The route Rose traveled on the way to buy her favorite sweets was the same she used to take a full thirty years ago, to and from her school. How early she'd had to get up! On winter mornings it had still been dark when she and her parents ate their breakfast in the small kitchen of their house in Troy Street. A tightness came into her chest when she remembered that table set beneath the window, just big enough for the three of them: Dad in his gray suit, ready for the office, his hair slicked back neatly behind his ears; Mum in her red silk dressing gown. How young they'd been! Rose marveled—not that she'd realized it then.

I'm an orphan, she thought, and almost smiled, because the word seemed ridiculous applied to her—a small woman with graying hair who'd be forty-five her next birthday. Her mum and dad had been in their late thirties when they'd drowned, both of them, together, in a ferry disaster in Malaysia, visiting the town where they'd been born. Rose hadn't gone with them, it was too close to her first-year exams at the university, and she was old enough, they'd all agreed, to stay home by herself. "Next time," Mum and Dad had promised her. "We'll all go when you finish your degree." But there never was a next time, and Rose had never finished her degree. The high marks she'd earned in those first exams had seemed like a taunt to Rose. Her friends had been afraid to congratulate her—how could you congratulate a person whose parents had just died?

The train slowed, brakes squealing. Rose got up from her seat and walked up the aisle and through the doors into the glittering morning. Then up the steps and down the ramp, across the road and around the corner into Good Street toward the white façade of Lakshmi Palace of Sweets. The shop hadn't been there in her parents' time; her mother's love for gulab juman was a memory of her own childhood in Malaysia, when her grandmother had bought them from the Indian shop every year as a birthday treat.

How astonished Mum would be, thought Rose, to think that she could actually buy them here, in this old Australian suburb, which, back then, had been a place where the tastes of other countries were unknown. Rose gazed through the window at the gleaming trays of jalebi, sandesh, rasgulla, barfi, ras malai. If Mum were alive today, they would have made this little trip together. They would have—Rose checked herself. Mum wasn't here, and that was that.

Only it wasn't, really, because you kept remembering, and what she remembered most from that summer of her parents' death was the aching loneliness, the hollow sense of absence, as if a real physical space had been carved out beneath her ribs. And this hollowness was echoed by her footsteps on the shiny wooden floors of the empty house where the three of them had lived together, and later, when the house was sold, in her small flat near the library school. Rose shivered. *Tock tock tock* on a summer's evening: for her that had been the very sound of loneliness. And because she had never seen the place where her daughter now lived, Rose feared such loneliness for her. She swallowed. It was three whole weeks since Rose had heard from Clara.

22 FIRST QUARREL

Clara and Lonnie were having their very first quarrel. It sprang out of nowhere, like a small violent cloud on the edge of a pure blue sky, so small that at first you barely notice it— only when you look again, that little cloud has covered half the sky. They were sharing a bucket of chips on the lawn of the Eastern Quadrangle, the place where Jessaline had first glimpsed Clara with her boyfriend. Now Jessaline saw them again as she passed on her way to the bus stop, the bus that would take her to David Jones Food Hall in the city, where she would roam happily all afternoon, skipping her classes and gazing at exotic foodstuffs instead, planning menus for the restaurant she hoped to have one day. Wandering DJ's was homework, really, Jessaline told herself, homework for her new career in Hospitality.

She waved, and when Lonnie and Clara failed to notice her, Jessaline didn't feel the least bit neglected, as she might have only a few short weeks earlier. Once you got a life, reflected Jessaline, you didn't have time to feel touchy or paranoid. "Once you get a life," she hummed, "a life, a life ..."

The quarrel hadn't quite begun as Jessaline passed by. Clara was telling Lonnie about the problem she had with her mum. "She wants to see my room. She hasn't asked, but I know she wants to. And I should invite her, only—"

"Only?"

"It's like—like it's my own private place, and I don't want

family in it, not yet, not till I've got over them." Got over all those quarrels she'd had with her dad, she meant, and with her mother too, about the way Mum simply put up with stuff, so that even the sight of her mother's sad, quiet face could make Clara feel upset, and then enraged. In the peace of her room at Mercer Hall, she'd begun to get free of all that; she didn't want Mum coming there. "I feel sort of ... torn," she confided to Lonnie, and Lonnie understood exactly what she meant, because he felt torn, too. He was torn about Nan's party. He wanted to go for her sake and because he loved that little house up in the mountains, the pretty rooms he seemed to have known forever, the long lush garden with its views of blue ridges and endless sky, the hammock swung between the trees—it had been a good part of his life.

But how could you go to a party for someone who'd written you off? There was something implacable about writing a person off, something as cold and hard and glittering as the edge of Pop's stupid ax. Pop might not have cut his head off, but he'd wounded him all the same. Banished him.

"He goes over the forks," said Clara suddenly, and for a moment, because he'd been thinking of him, Lonnie thought she was talking about his pop.

"Goes over the forks?"

"My dad," she explained. "When Mum does the washing up. He goes over them to see they're washed properly. And if they aren't, if there's the tiniest little speck left there, then he makes her do it again. And she *shouldn't*!" exploded Clara, the old rage boiling up inside her.

"Forks," murmured Lonnie, and he smiled. He couldn't help it, this image of three grown people fighting over forks was laughable.

"What are you smiling about?" asked Clara in a low fierce voice he'd never heard before.

"Just, ah, you know, forks. It seems so—"

"Petty? To carry on about?"

"Um ..."

"What about your *ax*, then? Your pop's ax that you keep going on about?"

Lonnie's smile vanished. Forks were no match for Pop's ax: the glint of it, the sheer ugly *size*. "What about it?"

"Well, he's not going to cut your head off or anything, is he? He's this poor old man, almost eighty. He—"

"Poor old man?" Lonnie was incredulous. How wrong she was! The new gloss Clara's company had brought to his view of life hadn't extended to Pop. "He's worse than your dad any day!"

"Oh?" Clara seized his hand. "C'mon," she said.

"Where are we going?"

Clara wouldn't say.

Twenty minutes later, they were in the main street of a quiet inner suburb, half-concealed behind a skinny coral tree. "Now watch that door!" ordered Clara, pointing across the road.

"The brown one?"

It was a very narrow door, squashed in between a drugstore and a fruit seller's. Gilded letters on an upstairs window read: Charles M. Lee, Tax Accountant.

"That's your dad's office?"

"Yes." Clara checked her watch. It was two minutes to one. Abruptly, the brown door opened, and a stout bald-headed man, arms laden with files, burst out of it. He glared at a council rubbish bin, dropped the files inside it, kicked the bin sharply, and stomped away up the street.

"Your dad?" asked Lonnie.

"No," said Clara, adding impatiently, "how could he be?"

"Huh?"

"He's not Chinese, is he?"

Lonnie stole a quick glance at her. "Oh, right. Yeah. I forgot."

Clara grinned at him. "You're so—" A distant clock boomed out the hour. "Now!" she cried, and as the sound died away, the brown door opened again and a small slender man emerged, blinking into the sun.

"*That's* him." Clara grabbed Lonnie's hand, and together they followed the small man up the street.

"What if he looks around and sees us?" Lonnie said, sounding worried.

"He won't," said Clara confidently.

Half a block farther, Mr. Lee turned off the main street into a small paved square. He sat down on a bench and took a brown paper lunch bag from his plastic carrier.

"Ham and pickle," whispered Clara. "He always has the same. Sliced *very* thin. And if Mum doesn't shave it thin enough, she has to do it again."

Lonnie studied Clara's father. He looked so harmless, mild. "He's sort of ... small," he observed.

"Hitler was shortish," retorted Clara, and yet even as she said this, she was thinking how strange it was seeing her dad out in the world, away from home. If she'd been a stranger instead of his daughter, she'd have thought he looked lonely sitting on that little bench, lonely in the way a kid would look eating lunch by himself on the playground because no one would play with him. Serve him right! she thought, only then—perhaps it was the warmth of Lonnie's hand clasped in hers or the thought of her room, her own private place waiting for her at the end of a short bus ride, or her own life, full of promise—she didn't know quite what—but all at once Clara could imagine herself saying, one day, in a calmer, older voice, about her father: "He's not a bad old stick."

Could that be? Ever?

Lonnie was squeezing her hand. "We quarreled," he was saying. "We quarreled, Clara."

So they had. "It was a kids' fight," she replied and then waited, because perhaps he wouldn't understand what she meant.

He did understand. "Yeah, wasn't it?" he agreed. "Like: who's got the biggest bogeyman?" He squeezed her hand again.

She leaned forward and kissed him.

Emerging from the park where he always went to eat his lunchtime sandwiches, Charlie Lee saw his only child, his once-precious daughter, kissing a great Australian lout in the middle of the street. A long-haired lout, the sort who, Charlie knew, would, if employed at all, always be late with his taxes. He stood stock-still, his fists clenched by his side, waves of rage and shock rolling through his blood. This was what they left home for, he thought bitterly, these girls ... He wouldn't even tell Rose, he decided, crossing the road and striding down toward his office. He wouldn't tell Rose because what Clara did now was none of their business. She wasn't ... she wasn't their daughter anymore.

23 CHIKO ROLLS

Stan was raging. The blasted fish and chip shop had gone, a brash new computer store in its place! He walked the length of Good Street—as his mum had done, he remembered, trudging from one greengrocer's to another, looking for a penny off a pound of beans. Only Stan was looking for a take-out. And when he found one, it was the wrong sort. He realized this the very moment he entered the shop: posters with Chinese writing on the walls, and in the shining trays beneath the glass-topped counter, noodles and vegetables, bony objects in a thick black sauce, tiny white pasty things ...

The old woman behind the counter smiled at him. "Yes?" she asked. "Yes?"

Stan flushed and pointed to the pasties—they looked the safest. "Um, what's in those?"

Now it was Marigold's voice he heard in his ear, Marigold on what he always thought of as the Night of the Chooks' Feet—May's birthday, when Marigold had taken them to a big Chinese restaurant in town. She'd ordered the Banquet. Stan's fork—he'd refused the chopsticks—had hovered above his bowl. "But they're feet!" he'd protested. "Something's feet. I'm not eating feet!"

But he couldn't help noticing how May was tucking in quite happily, and Lily, and the boy who'd still been his grandson back then, so that Stan, fork down, arms folded sternly across his chest, had felt an odd little sense of being left behind.

"In these?"

Stan jerked back to the present, to the old lady behind the counter beaming at him, pointing to the pasty things. "In these?"

Stan nodded.

"Wegetarian."

They were out, then. After the shock he'd experienced—the place where he'd grown up vanished while his back was turned—Stan felt he needed meat. Meat of some kind, anyway. "Got any Chiko Rolls?"

"Ah, chicken!" She pointed to a tray of skewered meat. "Chilli or Satay?"

Stan didn't fancy either. "Not chicken," he said. "Chiko."

"Chiko?" She put her head on one side, eyes twinkling up at him. He had an uncomfortable feeling she thought he was a fool.

"A Chiko *roll*," said Stan. His mouth filled with saliva. Even to say the words brought the taste of chewy yellow batter and that unique and unforgettable gray mince. "You wonder what it is," May always said.

"They're yellow," Stan added helpfully. "Yellow rolls." He sketched a quick cylindrical shape with his old hands.

"Ah! Rolls!"

"Yeah? You've got some?" Stan felt an absurd pulse of relief, as if he'd feared even the food he'd once eaten might have vanished into history.

"Spring rolls! There!" She pointed.

"No, not spring rolls. Chiko."

She looked puzzled, and Stan's heart wasn't in it anyway. He knew there was no place left around here where you could get a decent honest Chiko roll. "Okay. I'll take two," he said, pointing to the spring rolls.

Outside in the street, he thought they tasted funny. "Okay, not *funny*," he said to an invisible Lily—or perhaps it was Lonnie, or Marigold, or May, all of them somehow eager to make out he was some sort of racist. "Not *funny*—different. Different to what I'm used to, to what I—grew up with."

"Grew up with!" He could almost hear Lily's contemptuous snort.

This trip back to the old place hadn't worked, he thought miserably. The streets he'd walked in with his mum had the same names, and that was about it; there was nothing left to jog his memory, nothing left to bring back her face and the forgotten color of her eyes, which had seemed so important for him to remember. Stan slumped down on a gray metal bus seat—they'd been made of wood in his day—and stared across the road, where a Chinese woman with a basket over her arm was gazing into the window of a big white sweetshop. As he watched, a plump tabby cat strolled from the doorway and weaved itself around her legs. Stan smiled to himself as she bent to stroke it, recalling how, seventy years ago, he and his friend Archie Lewis used to take the mickey out of old Jimmy Chan down at the fruit shop: "Fattening him up for Christmas dinner, eh Jimmy?" Arch would say as Jimmy stood on his doorstep with Snowball, his beloved white Persian cat, cradled in his arms, and Stan would join in with "Watch out, puss!"

Geez, they'd been a pair of rough little buggers. "Watch out, puss!" he chortled, remembering how Jimmy had called back to them, "I save you his tail, boys! Best bit!"

Across the road the Chinese woman turned from the sweetshop window and glared at him.

He'd said it right out loud! "Watch out, puss!" He must

have, and she'd heard, and perhaps she'd thought he was talking about her, warning the cat she was after him for lunch …

She must have, because now she was crossing the street at a pretty fast trot, heading in his direction, still glaring, coming after him—

Like the ten-year-old he'd been back in the days of Jimmy Chan, Stan sprang to his feet and bolted, down the street and around the corner, through the yard of the Baptist Church and then down the dark little alley that, mercifully, hadn't vanished with the rest of the place. Then out into the sunlight and the trampled scrubby grass of the park, he sank down, winded, on a bench, took a big checked hanky from his pocket, and dabbed it at his sweating face. Geez! he reckoned it'd been a full forty years since he'd run as fast as that. He glanced back toward the alley, only a perfunctory glance because the Chinese woman would never work out where he'd gone—you had to grow up around here to know about that alley.

But why had he *said* such a thing?

"Yes, why?" Lily's voice demanded in his head.

"Didn't mean to say it," muttered Stan. "Not out loud, anyway. I was just … remembering old times. Didn't intend that poor woman to hear." But—the look on that poor woman's face! Stan fought hard against a chuckle, swallowed it down. Thank God Lily hadn't really been here with him; he'd never have heard the end of it. "You're such a racist, Pop!"

Only he wasn't, really. Old Jimmy Chan had been a friend of his and Archie's, not that Lil would ever believe it. Hadn't they looked after Snowball that time Jimmy had to go off to Temora because his eldest daughter was having a baby there?

Looked after him really well, fed him cooked liver, fish heads, nothing but the best. And never—Stan couldn't stop the chuckle now, it burst up from his throat, set his whole body rocking—never said a single racist word to him.

"Aaargh!" Stan pressed a hand to his ribs; because a sudden pain had flowered there. Too far to the side to be a heart attack— that would be in the middle. A stitch, this was, he thought, a simple stitch from running, that was all.

Rose was furious. Absolutely furious. Didn't they ever learn anything, these old Aussie racists, with their red faces and bristly soldier's hair? Didn't they know you couldn't call out insults in the street?

Because that's what it was, for sure; she wasn't born yesterday. The kind of childish insult Rose remembered from her primary school because all the kids back then thought if you were Chinese, you ate cats—and rats, and dogs and spiders, though especially, for some reason, cats. Well, that was then and this was now, and the old bigot wasn't going to get away with it! She'd had enough: this was the twenty-first century, and she should be able to stroke a cat like anyone else, without having some backward old fool suggesting she was sizing it up for dinner. "Hey!" she called, though the old guy was already halfway down the street—heading for the alley, she'd take a bet on it! Rose smiled grimly. "Think I eat cats, do you?" she muttered, setting off in hot pursuit, around the corner, through the churchyard, down the alley, out into the park, where she spotted him at once. "You!" she cried, striding over the grass toward the bench. "Hey, you!"

When he looked up, his face was gray and she saw he was holding one hand against the side of his chest. At once Rose forgot about vengeance. "Are you all right?"

"Yeah." He took a deep breath. "Just a … bit of a stitch. That's all it is."

"Are you sure?"

He nodded.

Rose saw the color was coming back into his cheeks. He was all right. She could still have a bit of him.

"Run away too fast?" she said.

"Eh?"

"You heard me."

His color grew deeper. "Look, I—"

Rose could almost swear the scalp beneath his bristly hair was turning scarlet. All the same, he wasn't getting away with it. "Calling out stuff!" she scolded. "In the street! At your age! You ought to be ashamed."

"I know," he said, surprising her.

"You *know*? What kind of answer's that?"

"I'm sorry." Stan wiped the back of his hand across his flaming forehead. "I know how I sounded."

"Sounded? Making out I eat cats because I'm Chinese!"

"Ah no, it wasn't that. It was only, I was remembering—"

Suddenly it was all too much effort for Stan to explain. It would take an age to tell her about Jimmy Chan and Snowball, and Lily always saying he was racist, and the old place vanishing, like Chiko rolls and the color of Mum's eyes, and friends he'd grown up with, and Lonnie …

"Don't know what came over me," he said simply. "Saying stuff like that."

"Something stupid," the Chinese lady said to him, smiling, and then sitting down beside him, her eyes studying his face, she asked, "You from around here?"

"Not now," he said. "Grew up here."

"So did I. Born here," she told him, stabbing a small shoe into the dusty grass in front of their bench, as if she meant, *right there*, so that Stan imagined a tiny Chinese baby in a lacy shawl lying on the grass.

"Long time ago now," Rose sighed, remembering the little house on Troy Street and how her mum used to wait at the gate for her to come home from school. Too much had happened since then, so much she could never tell it all, though for some odd reason she would have liked to pass a little bit on to this dopey old Australian who'd grown up where she was born.

"Ah, you're a spring chicken compared to me," said Stan gallantly.

"Not so young. Got a grown-up daughter at the university. Clara." Rose's eyes filled suddenly with tears.

Clara. The name rang a distant bell for Stan. Where had he heard it recently? He stared out at the horizon and concentrated until it came to him: May calling out through the kitchen window while he was mowing the lawn. "Lonnie's got a girlfriend! She's called Clara."

Only this wouldn't be the same Clara, couldn't be ...

There was a small sniffling sound beside him; he looked around and saw that the Chinese lady was crying, big tears rolling from her eyes.

Stan was horrified. It was his fault, it must be. He'd upset her back there in the street. He took the big checked hanky from his pocket again. "Sorry," he blurted, pressing it into her hand. "It's a bit crumpled, and—look, what I said back there, um ... about cats—"

"As if I'm crying about *that*," she scoffed, dabbing at her eyes.

"You're not?"

"What do you take me for? I'm crying about Clara."

"She got a rubbish boyfriend?" Stan didn't quite know why he'd said that. Except, wouldn't Lonnie be a rubbish boyfriend?

The Chinese lady looked at him in surprise. "Boyfriend? I don't think so. I—oh, I wouldn't know. I wouldn't know anything, see? That's the trouble. She left home in the summer, and—" now she was in tears again, "—I've never even seen her room!"

"Her room?"

"In that residence hall, where she lives. I keep on worrying it's a lonely kind of room. You know, the sort that echoes ..."

Like Lonnie's place might be. "Well, go and have a gander at it then," he told her. "Set your mind at rest."

"She hasn't invited me."

There was no way in the world, Stan knew suddenly, that Lonnie would invite him over.

"That doesn't matter," he said stoutly. "You're her mum. You've got a right."

She looked up at him, and her big glossy eyes reminded Stan of his mum's. They had exactly that same bright soft expression, though they were a different shape and color. Mum's eyes had been ... a deep blue, almost navy, and other times dark gray, that color you saw in the sea on certain stormy days.

Like Lon's eyes.

Of course! Lonnie had Mum's eyes! How had he forgotten? Because Lon wasn't his grandson anymore, that's why! He didn't want to think of Lon; he didn't want to think he'd come all the way here because it was the color of Lon's eyes he was really trying to remember. Of course it wasn't; of course he hadn't.

Stan was glad when the Chinese lady touched his arm and asked, "You really think I've got the right? To go there? You don't think it would be … invasive?"

"*Invasive!*" Stan snorted. "Invasive" was the kind of word he'd heard from Lil and Lonnie. "Who do they think we are? The enemy?"

"Yes," she said simply, and they both laughed, and she handed him the checked hanky so he too could wipe his eyes, and Stan had the definite feeling that he'd made a friend.

24 THE DRAMA SOCIETY

Lily knocked on the door of the staff room and waited.

No one came.

She waited longer, a little uneasily for there were girls who developed crushes on teachers and came to the staff room door pretending they had homework problems simply for the delight of speaking to Mr. Hallam or Mr. James. Lily glanced nervously up and down the corridor. Surely no one could mistake her for that kind of person. After all, it was Mr. Corcoran she needed to see, and no one could suspect any girl, even a weird Year Eight, of having a crush on Mr. Corcoran, who was stout and middle-aged and quite bald except for those tufts of gingery hair perched over his ears. He looked like a drowsy old koala.

Mr. Corcoran taught drama, he ran the Drama Society, and he organized the school production.

Daniel Steadman was in the Drama Society; Daniel Steadman was playing Hamlet in the school production.

Lily knocked on the door again, and this time it opened, the merest little slit, and the cold gray eye of Mrs. Jossop, the phys ed teacher, peered out at Lily. "Yup?"

"I ... I'd like to talk to Mr. Corcoran," stammered Lily.

Ms. Jossop chuckled. "Really?"

"It's about the school production," said Lily quickly.

"School production, eh? Good excuse." Ms. Jossop winked at her.

"What?"

Ms. Jossop winked again.

"No, really," protested Lily. Was Ms. Jossop mad? Or was she simply joking? "Really, I want to ask him about joining up. I don't take drama so I couldn't ask him in class and—"

"Jerry!" Ms. Jossop hollered back into the room. "Fan of yours out here!"

A fan. Lily's face flamed. It was still flaming when Mr. Corcoran appeared at the door, wobbling a little as if his ample flesh hadn't settled from the effort of the stroll across the room. "Yup?"

Why did they all say "yup"?

"I'm Lily Samson, Mr. Corcoran, from 10B."

"Don't teach that lot."

"I know, Mr. Corcoran. That's why I'm here."

"Too late in the year to change classes."

"I *know*. I've come about joining the Drama Society and the school production. It says on the notice board: New members welcome."

"Old notice, that. Cast list for the production's already filled."

"Oh, I don't mean the cast, Mr. Corcoran. I meant, something sort of … subsidiary."

"Subsidiary?"

"Like … scene painting. Um, do you need anyone for scene painting?"

Mr. Corcoran thought for a moment, scratching at his orange tufts. "Year Seven has that pleasure. Thursday nights, it is, in the art room." He snorted. "Reckon their parents think they're safely down at the pub. You want to join in, you're welcome."

Year Sevens! Lily swallowed. Not even for Daniel Steadman would she spend an evening with Year Sevens! Besides, she wanted Wednesday afternoons in the school auditorium, when the play was rehearsing and Daniel would be there. "Lighting?" she ventured.

"Bunch of weirdos from Year Nine Advanced Science. Wouldn't recommend it, lassie. Not if you value your personal safety."

What did that mean? Lily knew she didn't want to find out. "Well, perhaps I ..." she tailed off, noticing uneasily that Mr. Corcoran was staring at her. Male teachers of Mr. Corcoran's age always made her feel uneasy; her dad had been a teacher. That's where her mum had met him, when they were both at Teachers' College, before her mum had changed over to psychology. If Mum had studied psychology before she'd met Oliver DeZoto, would she have married him? Lily had no idea, but whenever a male teacher of middle age stared at her she half expected him to say, "Lily Samson? I was at college with your dad." Then he might start telling her all kinds of stuff she really didn't want to know, because why would you want to know stuff about someone who'd left home before you were even born?

All Mr. Corcoran came out with was, "Say that again."

"Say what?"

"What you last said."

"I can't remember what it was."

"Say anything."

"But I don't—"

"That'll do!" Mr. Corcoran held one hand up, like a policeman. *What* would do? Lily didn't like to ask because she thought he might be even madder than Ms. Jessop; there was a high breakdown rate among the teachers at Flinders Secondary. His eyes were gleaming, and she wanted to run, only she felt instinctively that this might not be wise. He was probably manic, like Mum said old Mr. Roberts was when he'd stolen her yellow dungarees and wandered out into the street. Lily stood very still.

"Perfect!" he exclaimed.

"Perfect?" she whispered.

"I've got just the spot for you, girlie. In fact, you're exactly what we need."

"For what?"

"The school production."

"But I thought you said there weren't any places left."

He waved her words aside. "School auditorium. Three fifteen. Be there."

She was there on the dot. She caught a glimpse of Daniel, and the merest glimpse was enough to send that weird fizzy feeling sparking through her veins; the floor seemed to sink away, as if she were floating in the air. Daniel himself stood firm upon the stage, close to the tall, skinny girl from Year Eleven who played Ophelia, their heads bent over their lines. For a few seconds, hope as well as jealousy surged up warmly in Lily's breast. Could that be what Mr. Corcoran had meant when he'd said, "You're exactly what we need!" Could he want her for Ophelia's understudy? And then the tall girl, who was pale as well as skinny, might catch glandular fever and have to stay in bed for months and then—even as she had this pleasing thought, Lily knew it couldn't be. Only a blind person would choose a squat plump girl with frizzy black hair to understudy Ophelia, and despite his pebble glasses, Mr. Corcoran wasn't blind.

"Ah, Lily, here you are." Mr. Corcoran thrust a battered copy of *Hamlet* into her hands.

The script? Lily's heart began to throb so loudly she felt sure the teacher would hear it. Was he blind after all? Was she really understudy then? Or had he found another part for her, one he'd forgotten that he hadn't cast? Hamlet's mother?

"Come along." Mr. Corcoran seized her arm and led her toward the stage. Daniel Steadman's gaze lifted from the script and swerved toward her. Or did it? Perhaps he was looking at Mr. Corcoran.

"Down here." Mr. Corcoran led her though a small door Lily had never noticed before, set into the side of the stage. Down five steps—"Mind how you go!"—into a tiny boxlike room with a wooden chair in its center and a tiny slit in the ceiling. Through the slit Lily glimpsed Daniel's strong ankles above his school socks and the Year Ten Ophelia's anorexic feet in ballet shoes.

"You're absolutely perfect," Mr. Corcoran growled at her.

Lily backed away.

"The perfect voice," he told her, pointing at the script in her hands, "for our prompter. Soft but carrying, clear as the proverbial bell."

Prompter!

"Sit down," said Mr. Corcoran. "Take the weight off your feet." He flipped through pages. "Act 3, scene 2—that's where we are today."

Daniel wouldn't see her, then. No one would see her down here. He'd hear her voice, that was all. And she'd hear him and see his feet.

That would have to do.

 MAY'S DAY

Lily thought her nan was the softest person she'd ever come across, so she'd have been surprised to see the steely glint in May's eyes this morning as May toiled up the hilly streets toward the gorge in the company of her imaginary companion. There was a big green shopping bag hanging from her arm, and you could tell it was heavy from the way May's right shoulder pulled downward and how she had to pause from time to time to take a breath and switch the bag to her other hand.

"I've made my mind up, Sef," she said, puffing. "I'm absolutely set on it. I'm having this party, and Lonnie's coming to it, and I don't care what Stan says."

The funny thing was, though, Stan hadn't said a single word—not yet, anyway—about Lonnie being forbidden to come. "Forbidden," snorted May. "Just let him try!" As if she'd let Stan get away with something like that! Neither had he threatened to go out if Lonnie was coming, as he did when May had Mrs. Petrie and a few other lady friends to lunch. No, except for complaints about the smell of glue (May was making all the place cards and invitations) and the sandy bits of party glitter that had got between the sheets, Stan hadn't said anything much about the party.

"Lonnie's *coming*," repeated May, and then she added softly: "Too many people have been lost."

First there had been her own unknown mother, whom

May always pictured as a thin, dark-haired girl creeping away across the lawn of the children's home and vanishing into a dark bank of trees. And Stan's dad had died from influenza, and then his mum the year after their wedding, and later on, poor old Emmy, before she was barely sixty. Then there was the second child she and Stan had hoped for, and who'd never come along, so that May always thought of him (she was certain he'd have been a boy) as getting lost on the way to be with them. There was Marigold's husband, too—though even May felt Oliver Dezoto didn't really count.

They were such a *small* family—they couldn't afford to let any single one of them get lost. And getting lost was easy. May remembered Stan's mum telling about her own brother Joey: how, when he was fifteen, Joey had a row with their dad and left home. He'd gone up north to work. Letters came at first, and then the spaces between them grew longer and longer until there was only space. "It's the strangest thing," Stan's mum had said to May, "all that growing up me and Joe had together, the secrets we had, and now, he's vanished—if I passed him in the street I probably wouldn't know him ..."

That wasn't going to happen with Lonnie. Lonnie wasn't going to vanish; he was coming to her party; and he and Stan were going to make up and stop their silly nonsense. The making up might even be happening already, because although she hadn't said so to Stan, May had hopes about his trip into town today. His train would pass the station where Lonnie lived, Stan would see the sign—Toongabbie—and he'd soften. He might even get out and find his way to Lon's boarding house and make up right away. Well, he might. "It's possible," she said to Sef. "Anything's *possible*."

Sef herself had vanished, a long, long time ago. May could

137

still remember the morning her friend had disappeared: how she'd woken and found Sef's bed empty beside hers, the blankets gone, the gray mattress with its pattern of black stripes quite bare. "Where's Sef?" she'd asked the other big girl, Dolly.

"Gone."

"Gone where?"

"She got adopted!" said Dolly excitedly. "And I think—you know what? I think by someone grand! Because she was so pretty, anyone would want her. Even ... even the king and queen!"

They all hoped for this, secretly: to be taken by someone *grand*, by kings and queens or movie stars—even a prince and princess would do.

How old would Sef be now? At the Home she'd seemed a big girl, but May herself had been so small that a girl of six would have seemed big to her. Suddenly, with great clarity, she remembered standing beside Sef at a window looking down on children playing in the yard. May had needed to stand on tiptoe to see from that window; Sef had simply stood. Sef wore a green dress with buttons on the shoulders. When May had leaned against her, the buttons pressed into her cheek. So she'd been only a head shorter. Two years younger, perhaps. Seventy-eight then, thought May, who would be seventy-six next November. Sef would be about seventy-eight, and unless you were unlucky, as Emmy had been, seventy-eight was no great age these days, so, somewhere, Sef might still be around. If they met in the street, would they know each other?

"'Course we would!" May puffed, pausing to switch her big green bag to the other hand. "We'd know each other any old age!"

This part of the road had been a bumpy bush track fifteen years back when Stan had retired and they'd moved up into the hills. Now it was tarred and level, and the houses beside it were brand-new, with pointed gables and sleek stone columns by their doors. Huge houses they were, two stories, even three—greedy houses, thought May, picturing with affection her daughter Marigold's little house, ancient and tumbledown. A dump, Stan called it, and May had to admit that she didn't like to stay there overnight; there were things in the walls, nasty scuttling things that Marigold said were possums and May feared might be rats. All the same, Stan shouldn't keep threatening to burn it down.

"Of course your pop won't burn it down!" she'd reasoned with Lily. "Of course he wouldn't!"

"He showed me the matches!"

Matches. May had tried unsuccessfully to suppress her smile. It would take more than matches to burn down Marigold's place; even at the height of summer, the dampness inside was palpable.

"What are you smiling at, Nan?" Lily had demanded furiously. "It's serious!"

"Your pop's all talk," May had told her. "All breeze and bluster. You should know that by now."

Apparently, she didn't. Now Stan *was* noisy, even May admitted that, and he seemed to have a funny knack of striking on the children's nerves with his boxes of matches and his ax—

"I bet that ax gives Lonnie nightmares!" Lily had chided her. "I bet he'll never come up to your place again. Never ever!"

"Your pop wouldn't hurt Lonnie, love. Even if he was angry."

"He lifted that ax, didn't he? Over Lonnie's head? His hands are trembly, Nan. What if he'd dropped it?"

Lily had a point there, May had to admit; Stan's hands *were* getting trembly.

So here she was, this bright blue morning, on her way to get rid of Stan's ax.

Down the gorge.

The big houses were thinning now, only one more left before the road became a track. "Nearly there, Sef," she said, plunging into the brush, and she thought she heard the faintest tremble in the air, as if Sef was really there beside her and had taken a breath to reply. May paused to listen, but there were only the sounds of magpies caroling and the usual tiny noises of the underbrush. She walked on to the lookout, lowered the big green bag, took out the ax, and walked with it right up to the edge. She looked down; beneath her lay a sea of mist, white cottony waves that rolled up toward the sun. May lifted her arm and hurled the ax from her. She saw it glint once as it went down, heard it clang against a rock, another rock, another—and then there was a moment's silence until the final, faintest *chung,* a sound as small and harmless as a pebble flung into a stream. "Gone," said May with satisfaction, wiping her hands along her skirt and brushing the last traces away. "Now we can have a perfect, cloudless day."

26 THE GIRL IN BLACK

Stan's homeward train was a late train because he'd had to pick up party stuff for May in town: dampness-resistant streamers—"just in case, though Sef and I are almost sure it will be a perfect day"—and more of that darn glitter stuff that got everywhere, in your bed and in the sugar bowl and even in your whiskers if you hadn't got around to a shave. It was a train that stopped at Toongabbie. Stan saw the sign slide by the window and remembered that this was the suburb where Lon lived now—how could he not remember, when May had stuck the address up on the fridge door so that he saw it every time he went to get the milk for tea? *Lonnie: 5 Firth Street, Toongabbie.*

But Stan didn't soften, as May had hoped he would: he didn't leap up from his seat and hurry out onto the station and then on down the street, searching for his grandson's new home. All that happened was that Stan gave a guilty start and turned his head away. Then he got mad. Because why should *he* be feeling guilty? He hadn't done anything to be ashamed of; *he* wasn't the one who couldn't stick to things, who worried his mother and drove her into tears. All the same, as the train pulled away from the station, Stan gave in a little—he turned back to the window and pressed his forehead to the glass almost as if he half expected to catch a glimpse of the boy who used to be his grandson walking down the street. But the window was dark, and all he could make out, behind the reflection of his own old face, were lines and lines of lights.

When he'd been Lonnie's age, this place had been all paddocks, country; now the train rushed on through built-up suburbs as the city spread farther out. Here was Pendle Hill, now Blacktown—and at Blacktown a young girl boarded the train. She came through the door at the end of his carriage, and she was dressed all in black. That was all Stan registered at first, the dusty crumpled black a lot of young girls wore these days—a couple years back even Lily had worn it for a little while—as if they were in mourning for something, Stan thought irritably, when they hadn't even lived. He leaned his head back against the seat and closed his eyes until he heard a man say sharply, in the kind of voice you wouldn't even use on a dog, "Go away!"

Stan's eyes snapped open. Farther down the carriage the girl in dusty black was standing silently beside a seat, her hand held out.

A beggar.

Stan hated that, simply hated it, especially when the beggar was young. It made him cringe inside.

"Go away!" said the voice again, and the girl moved on without a word. At the next seat Stan saw a hand reach out to her. Money was passed over. Good, he thought, good! And then there were no other hands held out to the poor kid, all the way down to him. He reached for his wallet, took out a five, then changed it to a twenty when he saw her face because she was so bloody young, this one. Her face was grubby in the way he remembered Lonnie's being grubby, years back, when he'd been a little kid. There was a cardboard sign hung around her neck, like a child in a primary-school tableau.

"*I am sixteen and pregnant,*" Stan read. "*My first baby is in care, and I have no home and family. I am—*" the ink in this last sentence had been smeared so badly he couldn't make it out. He could see the small mound of her stomach beneath the flimsy cotton dress, and it made him mad, bloody stinking mad. The whole thing made him mad.

Sixteen. The same age as Lil. Only Lil could never come to this. Lil was strong, and she was fortunate. This kid would have been—what?—fourteen when she'd had the baby who'd been taken into care, and now there was another one on the way. So what had happened to this girl's parents? Kids themselves, perhaps. And the grandparents? Why hadn't they looked out for her? Stan shifted uncomfortably in his seat. They would have been old enough at least. Written her off, that's what they'd done. A shiver ran right down Stan's spine.

The girl was beside him now; he handed her the twenty, watched her grubby little fingers slip the note safely out of sight and watched her walk on down the carriage without a single word.

"Shouldn't have done that, love."

"Eh?" Stan looked round. Two old biddies across the aisle were shaking their heads at him.

"Eh? Done what?"

"Given her money. She gets on here every day, see? Well, every day we go into town anyway." She turned to her friend. "We always see her, don't we, Dawn?"

Dawn nodded. "Her and others like her. On at Redfern, off at Parra, on at Blacktown again—it's her little business."

"Business?" echoed Stan faintly. "*Business?*"

"She's on the dole, or something like it. They all are, but

it's not enough, see? Not enough for the drugs, so they get up this little business begging on the trains—"

"And outside the malls, and down the quay—"

There was a kind of roaring in Stan's ears. He knew their type: they'd been around in Mum's days, and they'd be around in Lily's. They'd be around until Judgment Day. He remembered how Mum used to give him the once-over before he went out into the street to play, checking he had shoes on, putting the washcloth to his face. "There!" she'd say, "That's better. Can't have some old biddy reporting us to Welfare." The old biddies hung over their gates and judged the neighborhood; they didn't miss a trick. And Mum had been a woman on her own, two kids to bring up ...

Stan glared across the aisle. "Tight-arsed bitches!" he felt like roaring. "Bet ya still got your lunch money from school!" Instead he thought of May and took a deep, deep breath, and when he spoke, it was to say something May would have thought even though she might have been too polite to shout it at them, right out loud and in their faces as he did. "Haven't you any hearts?"

Gotcha! he thought, watching their necks and faces mottle, the looks of shock and outrage turned upon him. The one called Dawn made a choking noise deep in her throat. Her friend gasped, "Well! *Some* people!"

If this had been a swanky train, some first-class sleeper off to Perth or Melbourne, those two would have pressed a button and have him slung right off, but that wasn't something you could do easily on the 5 p.m. to Penrith and the hills. Stan glanced down the aisle, hoping the girl might have heard, but she'd gone upstairs. He could see her standing waiting by the door. It was raining out there; thick teary drops were sliding down the window. She had no coat; the black dress wouldn't keep out a good dose of May's foggy foggy dew …

Abruptly, the girl in black began to make sounds. They were terrible sounds, thick and guttural, echoing through the suddenly silent carriage as the train slowed, sliding into a station, past benches and signs and an empty waiting room, as if some poor tormented animal had suddenly found its voice. Stan knew at once the girl was deaf and dumb. He knew because of that friend Marigold had had in kindergarten; he recognized the thick loudness and the desperate-sounding urgency.

Across the aisle Dawn and her friend were clucking their tongues.

"Can't you see the poor kid's deaf and dumb?" he shouted. "Can't you understand?"

The train had stopped. She was on the platform now, her dusty black skirt spotted by the rain. For some reason he thought of Mum's old wedding dress hanging safely in the hall cupboard up there in the hills. He thought of its color— that soft creamy white that reminded you of kindness—and the way, when you looked at it, the dress seemed to shed a light; it was as far from that girl's dusty black as anything on earth could ever be.

Stan scrambled to his feet and headed for the doors. He was too late. With a snap and a jerk they closed right in his face, and the train began to move away. Anyway, what had he thought he was going to do? Take her home to May? Or to Marigold? He stumbled back down the rocking corridor and sat down again.

Where would a girl like that live? In some kind of hostel? In a shack? For a little while, until they'd found out about the boarding house, May and Marigold had worried that Lonnie might be living in a shack, and the idea always made Stan think of stink and toilets filled in with cement, of scurrying scabby rats and broken glass scattered on the floor. Lonnie was all right. Lonnie lived at 5 Firth Street, Toongabbie, and he had a family. If things went wrong, he knew they were there; he knew, whatever the quarrels, that they'd help him out. Sure he knew. He *should* know, anyway. If he had any sense.

It was that poor girl who probably lived in a shack. Or in a cardboard box down some dangerous back alley—he thought of the big black spots the rain had made on her dress and an old phrase of his mum's came into his mind: "It shouldn't be allowed!" No, it shouldn't, thought Stan. He closed his eyes, but the image of sodden cardboard wouldn't go away, and all the way to Penrith, across the river, up into the hills, the wheels beneath him rang and clanged, sounding out his mum's old protest: "It shouldn't be allowed!"

27 SEVENTEEN PAIRS OF SCISSORS

A week passed and the weather grew warmer; up in the hills the blossoms fell from the apple trees, showering Stan's lawn with small pink petals like confetti.

Jessaline and Mrs. Murphy made frangipani tart in Mrs. Murphy's kitchen. Clara and Lonnie took the ferry out to Manly and walked along the beach to Queenscliff, warm hands clasped, certain they were in love. Clara's mother resolved that if she hadn't heard from Clara by next Thursday, she would go quite uninvited to visit her daughter's room.

Wednesday came around and brought Lily's second visit to the Drama Society and the school production.

She almost didn't go. That morning she'd encountered Daniel Steadman walking slowly across the upper playground toward the library; she'd glanced at him as they passed each other, and he'd actually shivered. Or had it been a shudder?

A shudder, perhaps, because in the washroom at lunch-time, Tracy Gilman had said to her, "You smell really funny today. You know?"

"Funny?"

"Yeah." Tracy came closer, sniffing at the air round Lily. "It's like—like the water vegetables get boiled in? You know?"

Lily did know. It was her turn to make dinner, and knowing she'd be home late because of the rehearsal, she'd got up early and made a stew. She'd boiled vegetables ...

When the bell sounded at 3 p.m., she rushed to the showers

and scrubbed herself all over—and then she smelled rankly of school soap, and her hair had fizzed from the steam, and so she almost didn't go to the rehearsal ... until she'd realized how the tiny cave of the prompter's box would hide her from Daniel's sight and sense of smell.

Daniel hadn't been there.

"Daniel Steadman!" Mr. Corcoran had yelled out from the stage. "Daniel Steadman!" And then, looking around at them all, "Does anyone know what's happened to Daniel today?" There weren't many Year Elevens in the school production— only Daniel and the skinny girl who played Ophelia, and a few minor characters, two soldiers and a gentleman. Ophelia told Mr. Corcoran she didn't share any of Daniel's classes on Wednesdays, and the soldiers and the gentleman had been off at the soccer match against St. Xavier's all afternoon.

No one knew what had become of Daniel, except perhaps for Lily, who felt uneasily that he might have stayed away because of her, that he'd noticed she had this stupid crush on him, seen her walking past the senior common room, noticed the way her eyes flickered toward him, and was keeping out of her way, the way Simon Leslie kept away from poor jogging Lizzie.

Perhaps he'd asked someone about her, someone like Tracy Gilman. "Lily?" Tracy would have exclaimed incredulously. "Lily *Samson,* do you mean?" Then she'd have rolled her eyes. "Lily Samson's *weird.* Her whole family's weird—what there is of it. You know her dad ran away? You don't? Well, he ran away before she was even born. There used to be a loony sort of brother, but now he's run away as well, and they live in this awful old dump down the street from us. It looks just like the Witch's Cottage, honest! You should see the grass in their front yard. It's up to their knees. My mum says she's going to call the council if they don't take care of it soon. Then there's all these gross old people her mum keeps bringing home ... *funny* old people." Lily could just *see* Tracy's fat finger twirling at her forehead. "I reckon Lily Samson's mum works in a loony bin."

"What?"

"You *bet*." Now Lily could almost hear Tracy chuckle broadly. Then she'd dig Daniel in the ribs—Tracy was a rib-digging kind of girl. "She does all this housework, too."

"What?"

"Yukky old cooking and cleaning and stuff. Haven't you noticed how she smells of old dishwater, and ... and onions and boiled cabbage? If Lily Samson gets keen on you, do this!" Here Tracy would hold her nose. "And then, start running!"

No, of course they hadn't been talking about her. Of course they hadn't. Daniel wouldn't ask Tracy about her; he wasn't interested enough, except to shudder when he passed her in the quad, and perhaps that shudder had been about something else entirely, like a math test he'd forgotten. As for Tracy, she was always talking to boys—chatting them up, she called it, or trying out her hand. Mostly, they walked away.

But what if Daniel—

No, stop, Lily told herself sharply. Stop right there. Of course Daniel hadn't stayed away from the Drama Society because of her! How stupid could she even be to think so! What a long way she'd come since that morning in the kitchen when she'd imagined seeing Seely and then thought it might be a good idea to fall in love with someone! What a long way, and all of it downhill!

●●●

Peter Pianka took Daniel's part that afternoon. He made a rotten Prince of Denmark, curly-haired and chubby and cheerful, which wasn't how you thought of Hamlet, who would surely have been tall and slender and with a melancholy face like Lonnie's. Peter didn't know the lines, and Lily had to prompt until she was hoarse. He kept standing near her trapdoor, and her eyes fixed on his feet; he wore sneakers without socks, and his ankles were white and chubby, like a little kid's.

Because of all the prompting, the rehearsal ended late, and it was almost dark when Lily reached her front gate, where a single glance at the lightless house told her Mum was late as well. She mounted the shaky steps of their porch, swung open the rusty screen door, twisted her key in the lock, walked inside, and then, with a sickening lurch, was jerked straight back again, the strap of her schoolbag caught in the handle of the screen door. Struggling to free herself, Lily tore two fingernails; they looked so ragged and disgusting she almost sobbed aloud. All right! Slinging down her bag, she headed for her room, grabbed her nail scissors from the tray on the dressing table, and sat down on the bed. The moment she opened the tiny silver scissors they fell apart. She flung the two halves on the floor. All right! It didn't matter; they had plenty of other scissors in the house.

Seventeen pairs, in fact. The last time scissors had gone missing—back when Lonnie lived at home and never put anything in its proper place—Lily had made her mother sit down at the kitchen table and count up all the scissors that they should have had.

Two pairs of nail scissors

Mum's good sewing scissors
Mum's ordinary sewing scissors
Two pairs of kitchen scissors
The economy pack of cheapos they'd bought the last time
scissors had disappeared
A *second* economy pack
It had added up to seventeen. Seventeen pairs of scissors!
So where were they, now that Lonnie wasn't here and everything should be in its proper place? Nowhere, it seemed—neither in the drawers and cabinets and boxes where they should have been, nor in the places where they shouldn't, like underneath the sofa cushions or up on top of the fridge.

The bathroom! Surely there'd be scissors there. Lily hurried down the hallway and flicked on the switch at the bathroom door. There was a brief blast of light, a small *pop,* and darkness followed; the bulb had gone. Halfway across the room she trod on something soft and sodden that drew from her a little scream of fright. Seely? No, of course it wasn't. Shifting her foot, Lily took a deep breath and worked it out: wet towels, that was all. Only how could there be wet towels? Weren't wet towels Lonnie's specialty? Hadn't she gone on at him about them, over and over again? And if he hadn't been to blame for them, if it was Mum who left them lying there, or even Lily herself, why hadn't he said? Why hadn't he, instead of leaving her, this very minute, feeling guiltily that she'd accused him wrongly? Abruptly, she remembered how he used to do her homework when she'd been in primary school. He never did his own, of course, but he'd done *hers.* Lily sat down on the damp towels and burst into noisy tears.

Now the phone began to ring. She jumped up and ran blindly through the door. She knew it wouldn't be Daniel;

of course it wouldn't be, yet all the same she ran, her heart thumping hard and fast, some kind of quivery expectation jumping in her veins. The ringing ceased as she was halfway down the hall. The answering machine switched on, and Lily stopped dead as she heard Nan's small voice: "Marigold! Lily! Are you there? No? Oh how I hate these things, hate them! Was that the beep?"

"No!" muttered Lily furiously, through clenched teeth. Why couldn't Nan, and even Mum, ever learn how stuff worked? Mum had confessed she was reluctant to turn on her computer at work unless her assistant, Leonie, was actually in the room.

"Can you pass on a message to Lonnie for me?" Nan's little voice went on. "Can you tell him that silly old ax is gone? Your pop's ax? And remind him about the party again. Tell him it will be all right to come. I'm sure we're going to have a perfect, lovely day—" Nan's voice cut out.

Lily dialed the number of Lonnie's boarding house. She didn't know exactly when Nan's party had become important to her, only that it had. She kept dreaming of Nan's garden, of flowers and streamers and fairy lights twinkling in the trees. And whenever she passed a house with balloons fluttering at the gate, her heart gave a tiny, aching lurch. Why shouldn't *their* family have one brilliant, perfect day? Wasn't such a day something everyone had a right to, a day you could always remember, no matter what happened to you ever after in your life? A *whole* perfect day?

That was the problem with the Samson family celebrations: they were never whole. They might begin well—even that day when Pop and Lonnie had quarreled had begun hopefully, with fine summer weather and the pleasure of seeing

Nan again, and the beautiful house and garden, and even, for a few moments, Pop. Then, always midway through the afternoon, there'd be raised voices, tears, and worst of all, thought Lily with a tiny shiver, that sudden small indrawn gasp from someone who'd discovered a secret that it was better they'd never known.

The phone in Lonnie's boarding house rang on and on. No one was at home, obviously; Lonnie was out with Clara, and all the other boarders would be out with their girlfriends, and the landlady out with a person Lily's nan would call her "gentleman friend." Lily was the only one who could always be found at home.

She slammed down the receiver and turned away. As she did, she caught a sudden, shocking glimpse of her face in the mirror on the wall. Oh—oh *God!* Her cheeks were bright red, her eyes had gone small from crying, small as black buttons and gleaming crazily. Her face had always reminded her of some other person's, someone she couldn't quite put a name to, whose identity was like a word caught on the tip of her tongue. Now she knew who it was.

Pop. She looked like Pop! Pop in a rage, red-faced, button-eyed—all she needed was the crew cut.

No wonder Daniel Steadman wasn't interested.

"I can't bear it!" cried Lily, and as if in sympathy, her knee began to itch. She bent and scratched, forgetting all about her jagged nails—that snagged. She felt a run starting—in her best tights that she'd worn especially for the school production, for Daniel Steadman, just in case he happened to notice her on her way to the prompter's box.

And he hadn't been there! Lily sank down on the floor and began to sob again. The front doorbell rang.

28 DANIEL BURNING

Daniel Steadman was burning.

Burning, burning.

He'd started burning in double chemistry that morning and feeling woozy, too, so that he'd wondered for a moment if he'd inhaled something poisonous in the air of Mr. Culloch's lab. But no one else had seemed affected. All the other kids looked ... cool and sort of separate from Daniel, as if he was standing behind a wall of glass. "Are you all right?" someone had asked, and Daniel couldn't tell who it was because his eyes had gone all blurry, and anyway the voice sounded a very long way away.

"Yeah, I'm fine," he'd answered because he hated people fussing, and saying you felt funny always caused a fuss.

"You all right?" someone else had asked, louder, and a face came close to him, a woman's face, the face of Mrs. Lodi, the school librarian.

Daniel had stared round blearily. He was in the library so it must be third period, and he was frightened that he had no memory of getting there. "I'm fine," he'd said again, and Mrs. Lodi had slapped her cool hand against his forehead as if she was his mother and said, "No, you're not. You're burning up," which was funny because although he'd been burning just a moment earlier, now Daniel was shuddering all over with chill. "I'm sending you to Mrs. Palmer," Mrs. Lodi had said.

Mrs. Palmer taught Home Economics in junior school, but

she also had a certificate in First Aid and was in charge of the school sickroom, small as a cupboard, underneath the stairs. Mrs. Palmer didn't ask if he was all right; she said, "What have we here?" the same thing she'd said to Daniel back in Year Seven Home Economics, when he'd opened the smoking oven to find his pizza on fire. Then she clapped her palm to his forehead as Mrs. Lodi had done. Her hand smelled of warm dough and some kind of spice; Mrs. Lodi's had smelled of paper and the kind of fishy glue they used in the library, a glue that Daniel's cat Ernestine loved. Ernestine had eaten the spines of *So You Want to Be an Actor* and *Contemporary Australian Drama*.

"You're coming down with something," Mrs. Palmer had decided. "Mum at home?" and Daniel had nodded because Wednesday was Mum's half day.

"Lie down for a bit," Mrs. Palmer had suggested, and Daniel lay down on the short little bed that must have been meant for Year Sevens because it didn't have room for his feet, and the next thing, like magic, he'd been in Mum's car heading down Millward Street toward Dr. Ryla's office.

"Chicken pox!" Dr. Ryla had roared. "We don't often see chicken pox on a strapping lad your age!"

Dr. Ryla's voice was so loud it had made Daniel's ears ring, and it must have penetrated the door of the office because when he and his mum had emerged into the waiting room there'd been smiles and giggles all around, and a tiny little kid had pointed at Daniel and bellowed, "You're not allowed to *scratch!*"

Mum had said it, too. "You mustn't scratch," she'd warned him the minute they got home. "Otherwise you'll scar."

"Scar?" That sounded terrible—like the Middle Ages, like

the Black Death—when all he had was a little kid's disease ...

Mum had nodded, scarily. "It leaves little pits in your skin," she'd said.

But how could you stop from scratching when your whole skin felt on fire? The itching had eased after Mum dabbed on lotion and Daniel had been able to get some sleep, but now, waking, he was on fire again. He raised a hand to scratch and saw, in the dim half light of the room—he must have been asleep for hours—that his hand had swollen, swollen so monstrously that it looked like a great red club, and his other hand was just the same.

Daniel screamed.

Footsteps sounded in the hall. The light flashed on.

"Are you all right?"

Daniel made choking noises. He tried to point to his hands, but you can't point when your fingers have disappeared.

"Daniel?"

He held up the big red hands.

His mother laughed. *Laughed.* Had the world gone mad or something? Or was he still asleep and in a nightmare?

"Oh," she chuckled. "Isn't that a good idea?"

"*What?*"

"Your old boxing gloves. To stop you from scratching. I dug them out of the cupboard when you were asleep and put them on for you!" She looked really pleased with herself, and though Daniel had never been a violent person, he really felt like killing her.

"Want anything?" she asked. "Want some scrambled eggs?"

The very thought made his stomach turn. "Not hungry," he croaked at her.

"Some junket?"

Junket? He hadn't eaten junket since preschool. Junket was a kiddy food, like chicken pox was a kiddy disease. If his friends at school found out he had chicken pox, he'd never live it down—they'd make chicken noises as they passed him in the corridor; they'd flap their arms like wings.

"How long does it last?" he muttered.

"The chicken pox? Or the itching?"

"Both."

"The itching should go away in a few days if you don't scratch. And you'll feel better, too."

"How long will I be home from school and stuff?"

"Two weeks."

"Two weeks!"

"If you don't scratch, that is." She smiled at him tenderly. "Sure you don't want anything. Some milk?"

"No. I mean, yes, I *am* sure I don't want anything. Especially not—" his stomach churned again, "—milk."

She laughed again. How heartless she'd become! Just because he had a kiddy disease. She'd giggled. He could almost hear her passing on the news to Dad.

"Juice?" she asked him sweetly.

"No!" he roared. "I don't want anything."

"All right," she said coldly. "There's water by your bed." She tiptoed to the door. "Shall I put out the light?"

"Yeah." Daniel took a sip of water from the glass and let his head fell back against the pillows. Two *weeks.* Daniel liked school; he'd be bored to death at home. And he was in Year Eleven; he'd miss things. Already, today, he'd missed a rehearsal for the school production—two weeks more and they'd get someone else to play his part.

• • •

Besides, there was another reason he didn't want to miss rehearsals—a wave of wooziness surged beneath his burning forehead—a special reason. Only what was it? He couldn't remember, except that it had something to do with a voice, a beautiful, beautiful voice.

Whose voice? Everything had gotten all vague and cloudy. Did chicken pox destroy your mind? Had Mum put something in that glass of water? Tablets from Dr. Ryla? The wooziness flowed over him. His eyes closed. In less than a second Daniel Steadman was asleep.

29 MARIGOLD WAS LATE

It was a quarter past six and Lily's mum was late. Marigold hurried into the washroom, fumbling in her handbag for lipstick, a comb, and blusher. Getting home late was one thing—getting home looking a wreck could bring on the kind of lecture from Lily that Marigold was tired of hearing: how Marigold was overworked and underpaid and should get herself a better job. "With your qualifications, Mum ..."

Marigold was in no mood for such a lecture this evening; she'd had a hard, exhausting day. Captain Cuthbert had asked her to marry him again and become quite touchy when Marigold had refused. Old Mrs. Nesbitt had wandered off, and it had taken the police the whole afternoon to find her. Then Mr. Roberts had mislaid his special coffee cup, the one his wife had given him for their last anniversary. Red in the face and shouting, he'd accused Mrs. Nightingale of stealing it, even though Marigold and the little circle of old people ringed round him could clearly see the mug-shaped bulge in the pocket of his old tweed jacket.

"It's there," Marigold had said gently. "It's in your pocket, Mr. Roberts."

He'd pulled the mug out and turned it wonderingly in his hands. "How did it get there?" he'd asked them. "How?" and the astonishment in his voice, the expression in his moist blue eyes had reminded Marigold of Lonnie when he was little—the time he'd touched the iron and burnt his fingers. "But it hurt!" he'd kept on saying in exactly the same wondering way. "Mum, it hurt!"

Then her mother had called again to remind her once more to tell Lonnie to come to Pop's party.

"So Dad's made up with Lonnie?" asked Marigold.

"Not exactly, dear, but—" here the line had crackled, her mother's voice slipping away into the void, and the door of Marigold's office had burst open and her assistant Leonie rushed in with the news that poor old Mrs. Nesbitt had been found. "At the crematorium, can you imagine, Marigold! The cops told me she was looking at the wreaths. 'Happy as a lark!' they said."

Now Marigold studied her face in the washroom mirror; she did look awful. She looked, as her dad would say, like something the cat had dragged in. Lily would say it, too. As she stroked on blusher and applied her lipstick, Marigold remembered how Dad had hated her wearing makeup when she was still in school so that, coming back from Saturday outings with her friends, she'd had to scrub her face in the ladies' room of the local railway station before going home for tea. How strange it was that now she was putting *on* makeup so that her *daughter* wouldn't grouse at her the minute she walked in through the door ...

"The evenings are drawing out, don't you think?"

Startled, Marigold looked toward the shadowy place at the end of the room, from where the voice had come. A tall old lady was standing in front of the last washbasin, surveying Marigold with glittering green eyes. She held a comb in one hand, and from the crown of her head, long rippling waves of soft white hair flowed down past her waist. She looked beautiful and unearthly, thought Marigold, like an elderly Rapunzel watching at the window of her tower. Who on earth? And then Marigold recognized her, recognized the smart navy dress the old lady wore, with its neat crimson leather belt and trim.

Mrs. Nightingale. She'd never seen Mrs. Nightingale with her hair loose before. Normally, she wore it in a braided coronet above her ears. What was she doing in here so late? "Haven't your children come to collect you?" asked Marigold.

Mrs. Nightingale placed her comb on the ledge of the sink and began to braid her hair. "Why should they do that?" she asked, and Marigold felt a twinge of panic. Was Mrs. Nightingale's memory beginning to slip? Was she back in the past, as so many of the day-care clients were, back in the time when they had been the ones who did the collecting, picking up the children who now collected them?

And where *were* Mrs. Nightingale's children? If they'd failed to show up and if everyone else had gone, Marigold would have to phone around, possibly even drive the old lady home. Bundling the lipstick and blusher and comb into her handbag, Marigold nodded at Mrs. Nightingale and hurried out into the waiting room. With a surge of relief, she saw the old lady's son seated with his wife in the armchairs by the coffee table. "Oh, hello," she said. "Your mother's in the bathroom if you're looking for her."

Sarah Nightingale nodded. "Fixing her hair."

Her husband looked up. "We know."

"Takes hours," said Sarah. "And she hates it if I try to help."

They were poring over more shiny travel brochures, Marigold saw. So they must have sorted things out then, about their second honeymoon. They must have worked out some kind of arrangement for Mrs. Nightingale.

"So you're going?" she said brightly. "On that trip in September?"

"Oh no," Sarah said bleakly.

"No?"

"There's Mum," explained her husband.

"Oh, sorry, I thought—" Marigold gestured at the brochures. "I thought you'd, um, found someone."

"Ah, no," said the son, whose name Marigold could never remember. Gerald? Randolph? Phillip? Yes, Phillip, that was it.

"But we like to dream about it, you know," Sarah said plaintively. "We like to look at the pictures ..." Her finger traced a curve of shining beach.

Look at the pictures! The words clawed at Marigold's soft heart. It was all so ... sad. "How long is this second honeymoon?" she asked. "Isn't it—really short?"

"A long weekend," said Sarah. "Three days in September."

Three days was nothing. Words rushed to Marigold's lips, words she'd promised Lily she would never speak again. "Look, if you like, your mum can stay with me."

Oh, Lily will be furious! fretted Marigold as she drove off down the highway. Lily would be tight-lipped. "But you promised!" she would nag. "And Mum, listen, proper psychologists don't do this!" (How Marigold hated that word "proper"!) "Proper psychologists don't bring their lame ducks home! Mum, it's unprofessional."

Suddenly—perhaps it was the exhausting day behind her or the dread of telling Lily or the image of Mrs. Nightingale's poor mousy daughter-in-law tracing the curve of that shining beach—an unaccustomed anger rose in Marigold's heart. One weekend. A long weekend in September—three miserly little days. Surely Lily could put up with that! Had she no compassion? No, she hadn't, Marigold decided. Compassion, to Lily, was simply being soft. "You're too soft, Mum," she was always saying. "You let people take advantage."

And yet Lily was a good girl. She was the sensible one in the family: never a moment's trouble at school, homework and assignments always done on time, and always helping with the housework, shopping and cooking—

But oh, she was bossy! So bossy and bullying, so certain she was right that sometimes she reminded Marigold of—face it, Lily reminded Marigold of Pop. They were as alike as two peas in a pod in the way they took up all the space around them, and other people's, too. All the oxygen, all the room for simple breath. Beside them, other people were like wraiths.

Marigold had planned to put off telling Lily about Mrs. Nightingale's staying with them. After all, anything might happen in the days before September. Now, she decided to tell her daughter the moment she reached home: no cowardly delaying, no being soft. I'll simply tell her, Marigold resolved, and that's that.

She drove faster, almost eager for the confrontation, sailing along—and in no time at all she was cruising into her drive. She wrenched out the keys, slammed the door, and hurried up the shaky steps to the porch, groping in her handbag for the separate ring on which she kept the house keys. They weren't there. Marigold leaned on the doorbell.

When Lily opened it, her mother saw she'd been crying. *Lily? Crying?* Lily never cried.

Lonnie! thought Marigold, with an icy clutch of fear. "What's happened?" she gasped. "Is it Lonnie?"

"Lonnie?" Lily raised a tear-stained face. "No, it isn't!" she shouted. "Why do you always think of *him*?"

"What is it then?"

Lily dissolved again into tears. "I've broken my nails and I can't find the scissors!" she bawled out. "I've a run in my best tights, and, Mum—"

"What?"

"Mum, I saw myself in the mirror, and I thought I looked just like Pop!"

Marigold put her arms around her daughter. "Of course you don't look like Pop," she lied, smoothing the wild corkscrews of Lily's frizzy hair. "Not a bit."

"Honest?"

"Cross my heart." Marigold smiled treacherously. "And there are two pairs of scissors—for emergencies—in that little basket on the laundry shelf." She patted Lily's back—and decided she'd put off telling her daughter about Mrs. Nightingale's visit ... for a little while.

Lonnie was off to the hills to make up with his pop. They'd driven him to it, all of them: Nan and Mum for starters, always on the telephone, urging him to make up with Pop so as not to spoil the party.

And Clara prodding him, too. "Go on! What's so scary? He's an old, old man."

"I'm not scared."

"Proud then. Too proud." She'd leaned toward him and tickled at his ribs. "Too proud to say sorry."

"Why should l? Why don't you make up with your dad, then?"

She'd laughed. "I might, when he's eighty."

Lily was worst of all. "I *want* that party," she told him. "I want it to be perfect, Lon—" There was such a strange urgency in his sister's voice that Lonnie had asked, "Are you all right?"

"'Course I am. Why?"

"You sound des—" Some instinct of self-preservation made Lonnie choke off the word *desperate*. "Er, funny," he amended, but she'd got mad with him all the same.

"I do *not*," she protested, and then her voice had dropped down to a whisper. "Lon, don't you ever feel you have a right to some kind of perfect, happy day?"

"Huh?"

"A *whole* perfect day?"

"Eh?"

He obviously didn't know what she was talking about, thought Lily, standing in the dark hall at home, with her back to the mirror so she wouldn't catch a disconcerting glimpse of her Pop-like face. No, Lon didn't know what she was talking about, and why should he? Lon probably had plenty of whole, perfect days with his lovely Clara, while she—he'd wreck the party, she just knew it. Or Pop would. "Oh, forget it!" she snapped at him.

"Why do I have to be the one to make up, anyway?" Lonnie sulked back at her. "I'm not the one who lost his block, I'm not the one who—"

He broke off, visited by a distant memory of Mum walking toward him through a door holding something wrapped plumply in a shawl. "Here's your little sister," she'd said. "Here's Lily."

Lonnie gave in. "Okay," he'd sighed. "I'll go and see him. All right?"

So here he was, in the steep back streets of Katoomba, in a midweek quiet so intense you could hear the tiny sounds of radios playing in back rooms, the clink of china, an old lady's voice asking, "Fancy a cuppa, dear?"

Pop's territory was a country of retired people, creaky old couples, ancient ladies whose husbands, as Nan put it, had "passed away." Pop wouldn't pass away—the phrase was too gentle for him. He'd go out roaring. "Kick the bucket," as Pop would say himself, and kick it noisily so it slammed against a wall. Or—the thought struck Lonnie surprisingly—Pop might go like Emily Brontë, refusing the doctor, refusing to lie down. And then, when he'd gone, Lonnie would miss him …

Miss him? Miss *Pop*? Surprised again, Lonnie realized that he would.

But making up with Pop wasn't the only reason he'd come up here to the hills. There was something else, a matter so embarrassing that Lonnie didn't even like to think of it because it made his skin grow hot and his blood feel curdly inside his veins. Lonnie stood quite still in the middle of the pavement and put a hand up to his burning cheek.

It was—it was how Pop could be a little reactionary sometimes. "Reactionary?" Lily always said scornfully when her brother used this word. "You mean racist, don't you?"

Clara wanted to come to Nan's party. And Clara was Chinese, and well, not to put too fine a point on it, *was* Pop racist? Lonnie didn't really know; those weren't the kinds of arguments he ever had with his grandfather. Dimly he remembered Nan once telling him how Pop had refused to go to the new dentist, Dr. Tsai. Was that because Dr. Tsai was Chinese? Or had there been some other reason? And would balking at a Chinese dentist mean that you might balk at a Chinese daughter-in-law? That is, if, say, one day, he and Clara decided to ... to get married or something.

Although he was in love, the thought of marriage, an engagement, or simply living together made Lonnie feel uncomfortable, not because he didn't want these kinds of commitments—of course he did—but because he could sense an invisible audience of people whose mouths would drop open in astonishment if he so much as whispered such intentions, who would exclaim: "*You?*" as if he was twelve instead of twenty-two.

They didn't matter, Lonnie told himself firmly. Clara was the only one whose opinion mattered, and if she felt the same way he did, then perhaps one day—here Lonnie simply couldn't stop from smiling. Only when that day came, would Pop be a problem because he couldn't cope with the idea of a "New Australian" in the family?

"For sure," Lily would say.

Lonnie wasn't quite so certain. What he thought was that you simply couldn't tell about people. People were mysterious. Look at sensible, hardheaded Lily: who could have imagined she'd get so keen about Pop's birthday party? And look at Dad: Lonnie always told people he couldn't remember his dad, and this was true, except occasionally brilliant little pictures would surface in his mind, pictures framed with feelings. Like—sitting on the rim of the ocean baths at Curl Curl, high tide, waves crashing in, snuggled up to someone whose big warm body curved about his own, someone who kept saying, "It's okay, Lon. It's *fun*. Nothing can get you. I'm here—"

That was Dad. Unless he'd dreamed it or made it up, and somehow Lonnie knew he hadn't. That was Dad then, when Lonnie had been little, and yet he'd left them, and now he was nothing more than an awkward voice on the telephone.

Yeah, people were the mystery of the universe. Who could tell how Pop would act when he met Clara?

"Are you all right, son?" An old white head was peeping around a screen door. "You've been standing there so long, I thought you might—"

"I'm fine," called Lonnie, smiling weakly. "Getting my breath, that's all."

"You're May and Stan's grandson, aren't you?"

"Yeah."

"They'll be that pleased to see you, love."

Well, Nan might be, at least. Lonnie turned the corner into Ridge Road, where he could see the house a little farther down, the neatly trimmed holly hedge, the wooden gate that squeaked familiarly when he pushed it open. His footsteps sounded so loudly on the path that he was reminded of that story Dad used to read to him when he was little: *"There came a soldier marching along the high road—one, two! One, two!"*

The front door stood open innocently to catch the sun. Was he in there? Pop? Would he come rushing at him? Roaring, "Out! Out! Out! You're no grandson of mine!"? Lonnie swallowed. At least Nan had got rid of the ax. He squared his shoulders, took a deep breath, thought of Clara and then of Lily's strangely yearning voice, and knocked on the side of the screen door. His nan's voice floated out to him. "Is that you, Mrs. Petrie?"

Mrs. Petrie was Nan's friend from down the road; it was the weirdest thing, the way they used each other's surnames though they'd been friends for fifteen years. Lonnie cleared his throat. "No, it's me, Nan. It's only me."

"Lonnie!" A blur of color rushed toward him up the hall. Lonnie gasped; his nan was tiny, yet the force of her welcome almost knocked the breath from him. "Lonnie! Oh, Lon!" She stood back and beamed at him, her face alight with joy. "Don't just stand there, love! Come in!"

From his dry throat Lonnie managed a single word. "Pop?"

"Your pop's gone into town."

"Ah—ah." Lonnie sighed. He could sense Pop's absence the moment he stepped inside the house; the rooms were quiet as milk. Even when Pop wasn't shouting or stomping, his very presence seemed to make a noise, a humming inside the air, like a firecracker waiting to go off. "It's his blood," Lily had told him once, "his blood fizzing in his veins."

Relief swept through Lonnie in a sweet full tide, even though Pop's being away meant he wouldn't be able to try to make things right, as everyone wanted him to do before Nan's party. "You're coming, aren't you?" she asked him, almost before he'd sat down. "To Pop's birthday party? You and Clara?"

Lonnie gazed at her. How did she know he had a girlfriend? How did she know Clara's name?

Lily, he thought furiously. Lily must have found something that time she'd come to his room. Or Mrs. Rasmussen, yarning to them all on the phone.

"Are you?" pressed Nan.

He smiled at her. "Sure. Sure we're coming, Nan."

"Let me show you something." She jumped up from her chair, hurried from the room, and returned a moment later with Pop's mum's wedding dress, the one he'd found in an old trunk down at the back of the shed. "Beautiful, isn't it?" she said, and Lonnie saw at once how perfectly it would fit his Clara, how she could have been made for it: those tiny sleeves floating at her shoulders, the wide band of embroidery cupping the delicate hollows at the base of her throat, the silk flowing like water over her breasts and hips and thighs. Made for her—except it belonged to Pop, and if Pop was a racist, as Lily said, then Clara would never get to wear it.

He cleared his throat. "Nan? Can I ask you something?"

"Of course, love."

"It's something sort of—personal."

"Lonnie, I'm your *nan*."

"Right. Well then, okay. Um." He couldn't bring himself to

ask straight out if Pop was a racist. How could he? Nan loved Pop. "Um, you know how Pop won't go to that new dentist? Dr Tsai?"

"Silly old thing," said Nan fondly.

"Dr. Tsai?"

"No, of course not. I meant your pop. Refusing to go."

"Oh. Why won't he, Nan? Is it because Dr. Tsai's Chinese?"

"In a way."

Lonnie's heart sunk. "What way?"

"Well, perhaps I shouldn't say this, perhaps it might sound funny to you—"

"No, go on."

"I wouldn't like you to take it the wrong way."

"I won't."

"Well, I think your pop's got this picture of Chinese people, as being ..."

"Being what?"

"Tidy," said Nan.

"Tidy?"

"Sort of very neat and clean and tidy, you know. And your Pop's old teeth, well, they're not a bit tidy, are they? I think your pop's embarrassed, really. He doesn't want to show them."

"Oh," said Lonnie, relieved yet none the wiser about how Pop would react to Clara.

"Any message for your pop?" Nan asked hopefully, as the afternoon drew on and it was time for Lonnie to leave.

"Um, yeah," said Lonnie, and then he just stood there in the doorway shuffling his feet, trying to gather his thoughts, to work out his feelings, find the words. "Tell him I'm sorry."

That was what he should say, obviously, since everyone seemed to expect it. But those particular words stuck in his throat; he couldn't get them out. And why should he? Why should he be sorry for being—himself? Because that's what it boiled down to, didn't it? When you thought about it? Apologize for being the sort of person who got on Pop's nerves?

He couldn't. He wasn't going to.

Only then he couldn't think of what else to say, and as he stood in the doorway with Nan gazing up at him, a whole life history of himself and Pop came surging into his mind—not simply that last afternoon when Pop had run off for his ax but all kinds of other scenes, like a film running on fast-forward: Pop stomping and raging, Pop being kind, Pop noisy, Pop quiet, Pop teaching him how to bait a fishing hook and how to shave, Pop sitting silently on the sofa the day his old dog Ratbag had died. And though it was years ago, Lonnie could still remember how on that day he'd wanted to say something comforting to Pop and couldn't because Pop's grief for the old dog had made Lonnie tongue-tied.

"Tell him," he said to Nan now, "tell him I'm sorry Ratbag died."

It took her a few seconds to remember. Ratbag had been Pop's dog, and Nan had had a few problems with him. She'd particularly disliked the way Ratbag had learned to open zippers, taking the metal tag between his teeth, pulling out the stuffing from cushions and armchairs, and scattering chunks of foam and cotton like big heavy snowflakes on the floor. "Ratbag?" she murmured, puzzled, and then, realizing, "Oh, *Ratbag!*" She stepped forward, enveloping him in a quick, fierce hug. "I'll tell him," she promised. "He'll be that pleased you remembered—" She stood back to look at him again, admiringly. "You're a good boy, Lonnie," she said softly.

"No, I'm not," he said crossly because, really, she was too soft on him; she always had been, and he wasn't yet quite sure he could live up to her opinion. "I'm not an angel fallen down from heaven, Nan."

"I know." She *winked* at him.

He couldn't believe it.

31 RATBAG

Later that evening, as Lonnie lay on his bed in the Boarding House for Gentlemen picturing Clara in Pop's mum's wedding dress—the wide band of beading firm beneath her throat, her sweet face above it smiling at him—the phone rang down in the hall.

Lonnie tensed; he wasn't psychic or anything, yet somehow he knew this call would be for him. It wouldn't be Clara, because she had a seminar tonight and wouldn't be able to call him until eleven, and it was only nine o'clock. Mum, then. Or Lily. He hadn't told them he was going up to the hills today, but that didn't mean they wouldn't call to check if he was *planning* on going there. "Mr. Samson! Telephone!" Mrs. Rasmussen called cheerily from the hall.

"It's your little sister!" she exclaimed with delight as he made his way down the stairs, as if Lily was some sweet little girl he'd been longing to hear from for weeks.

"Thanks," he mumbled, and Mrs. Rasmussen smiled and said, "Big Day coming up, eh?"

Big Day? Lonnie stared at her. "Big Day" was the term people used for weddings, wasn't it? How did his landlady know he'd been thinking—only thinking, mind you, of the possibility that he and Clara—when he'd finished his degree, of course, and found a job and Clara had finished her degree ... Forgetting about Mrs. Rasmussen, and the telephone, Lonnie drifted into hopeful reverie.

The landlady eyed him curiously. "Your sister," she prompted, and Lonnie, startled, peered all around the hallway, half expecting to see Lily standing on the red linoleum.

Mrs. Rasmussen pointed. "On the phone."

"Oh—yeah." Lonnie picked up the receiver, and the landlady retreated to her flat, leaving, Lonnie couldn't help noticing, her door just a tiny bit ajar. She knew all about him, he was sure: Mum and Nan, calling when he was out, getting Mrs. Rasmussen and finding a sympathetic ear, would have told her everything, starting with his babyhood, then up through primary school, Dad leaving, high school, dropping in and out of courses yet being a good boy all the same, an angel fallen out of heaven—all the way up to the quarrel with Pop and Pop's party—of course! That's what she'd meant by the Big Day, not he and Clara getting—well, not he and Clara.

Lonnie became aware of a violent quacking going on in his right hand. He looked down and saw the receiver clutched inside his fingers. He raised it to his ear.

"So have you?" a strident voice demanded. Lily.

"Have I what?"

"Thought about making up with Pop."

"Yeah."

"But have you actually *done* anything?" He could tell from her tone that she believed he only ever thought and never did.

"I went up there today," he replied coolly.

"You went up there? To Pop's place?"

"Yeah." He was pleased by her incredulity. She hadn't believed he'd be game.

Then she spoiled it. "And?"

Lonnie sighed. Lily always wanted action. Results. "He wasn't there."

"So did you leave him a message? With Nan? To say you were sorry? So we can—I mean, so Nan can have a *proper* party?"

"Sorry for *what?*" he felt like saying. "For being who I am? Or not knowing who that is?" Only that funny note in her voice whenever she mentioned the party these days—a sort of yearning, was it? Anyway, something vulnerable he'd never have expected from his sister stopped him. "I told Nan to tell him I was sorry about Ratbag," he said instead.

"Ratbag. All right. You said you were sorry you were a ratbag." There was a pause while Lily considered this. "Well, I suppose that might do."

"Ratbag the dog," he said. "Not me."

"What?"

She didn't remember. Of course she didn't. Ratbag had been a long, long time ago: those slow walks with Pop stopping to pick up the old dog and carrying him in his arms, Ratbag with one ear up and one ear down, silky soft ears he let you play with, like velvet in your fingers—all that had taken place when Lily was hardly more than a baby and Dad gone only a little while.

"Ratbag was Pop's old dog," he explained. And then, "Not me. I'm not a ratbag."

"Huh!" said Lily, and she hung up.

32 UNINVITED

Uninvited, Clara's mum was on her way to visit her daughter at Mercer Hall.

A tiny glimpse, that was all Rose needed, the smallest little peep at Clara's room. "I have a right," she told herself, recalling how the bristly-haired old fellow she'd met in the park had said the very same thing to her: "You've got a right!"

Even if she hadn't been invited.

Once Rose herself had lived in a single room. A sad little room with a camp bed, a table and a chair, and a bare wooden floor that had echoed so frighteningly. Rose needed to know that Clara's room wasn't like that; she needed to know, silly though it seemed, that Clara's room didn't have an echoing wooden floor. She needed to *see* it.

As she stepped out onto the platform at Central, that familiar scent assailed her: a mixture of dust and sunlight, petrol fumes, and the yeasty odor from the brewery beyond the railway lines. It swept her back to those first months after her parents' deaths; to Wednesday mornings after her early lecture in cataloguing waiting on this very platform for the train to take her back home, when that scent had seemed the very air of desolation. She was eighteen, and her parents' house belonged to her now, and she lived in one room of it, the tiny room at the bottom of the hall that none of them had ever really used. Rose had moved the junk out, leaving the old camp bed, the table, and the chair.

She'd closed all the doors in the house except for the kitchen and bathroom: the door of her parents' room into which she couldn't bear to look; the door of the living room, which frightened her; even the door of her own room, which had memories of Dad and Mum coming in to talk or say good night. Yet still there was always the sound of her lonely footsteps on the polished wooden floor.

It was loneliness she feared for Clara, thought Rose, as she stood in the cold windy space of Eddy Avenue waiting for the bus to the university; and yet, wasn't this fear ridiculous? Ridiculous, decided Rose, climbing the steps onto the bus, finding a seat halfway down the aisle, watching the drab inner suburbs roll by. Clara wasn't alone in the way that she herself had been. Clara wasn't orphaned; she had parents, even if she didn't like them very much. Clara hadn't been *left*; she'd gone off bravely, of her own accord. Leaving the bus, crossing the campus toward Mercer Hall, Rose felt soft and foolish. She wanted to turn and run. Only she couldn't, because up there, from the window of her high room, Clara might have seen her coming, and she'd see her turning back, scuttling away like a mouse in a nighttime kitchen when someone switched on the light. So Rose kept walking, bravely, up the path, across a courtyard, and in through the big glass doors of Mercer Hall.

In room 2009, Jessaline woke sharply, thinking Rose's knock was on her door. She thought it was her parents. "Oh!" she gasped and slid down beneath the duvet. She wasn't properly awake, and now she entered into nightmare territory: somehow, her parents had found out she was about to drop Linguistics. Perhaps one of their colleagues had spotted her on that afternoon she'd entered the Hinterland and made her way into the Cathleen Cuthbert School of Hospitality. They'd spotted her and *told*. And now—now her parents were here to put a stop to everything. They would sit by her bed and argue, they would disapprove, and if Jessaline didn't give in to them, they would get ... plaintive. Jessaline hated it when her parents got plaintive, when their voices sounded wounded, as if she, their only child, had done them wrong ...

Jessaline lay perfectly still beneath her duvet. If she played dead, they would think she wasn't there. Had she locked the door, though? Cautiously and very quietly, she poked her head out from the covers. Wide awake now, she realized with relief that the knocking came from Clara's door. She glanced at her bedside clock: 10:15. She'd gone to bed late, having spent the evening with Mrs. Murphy in her kitchen making macaroons. They'd turned out perfectly, light as little clouds. Now she'd slept in.

At 10:15 Clara would be gone. Jessaline reached for her dressing gown. Of all the students on the twentieth floor of Mercer Hall, she was the only one who bothered with a dressing gown. It was long and pink and woolly, the kind that little girls wear.

Clara was obviously not at home, and in a way Rose was relieved, because she felt sure her daughter would have scolded her for coming uninvited. Spying.

"But I'm not spying," Rose told herself. All she wanted was one tiny little peep, so she wouldn't keep on imagining that Clara's room was the counterpart of the one she'd lived in all those years ago. Cautiously, Rose reached out to the doorknob—perhaps Clara had left her room unlocked. The knob refused to move.

"Can I help you?"

"Oh!" Rose's hand jerked back from the knob. A big gawky child had appeared in the doorway of the room next door. She couldn't be a child, of course, not if she was at the university—it was simply the pink fluffy dressing gown and the way she wore her hair in braids that had given this impression, making the girl look like those small children Rose sometimes saw on her evening shift at the library, all bathed and dressed for bed the moment they got home.

"Are you wanting Clara?"

"Yes," said Rose, flushing from guilt, hoping the girl hadn't noticed her hand on the knob of Clara's door.

"You must be Clara's mum," said Jessaline, and then she wished she hadn't because the only way she could have known this was because the lady was Chinese. And that was sort of racist, wasn't it? Besides, she might not be Clara's mum; she could be her aunt or a second cousin or even, thought Jessaline desperately, a Chinese lady who had nothing to do with Clara at all.

"Rose Lee." Rose held out her hand, and the girl clasped it warmly. "Jessaline. Clara's got an early tute on Fridays, Mrs. Lee. That's why she isn't here. And then she goes to the library. Or sometimes, instead of the library, she goes out with Lonnie—"

"Lonnie?"

Oops! Too late, Jessaline remembered Clara's mum hadn't been told about Lonnie. "Did I say 'Lonnie'? Sorry, I meant, um, she goes out with some friends. Shopping and stuff, little things ..."

"Little things," echoed Rose. Lonnie. So Clara had a boyfriend; she could tell it was true from the guilty expression on this nice girl's shiny face. A boyfriend she didn't want her mum to know about. "You're doing the same course as Clara?" she asked.

"Oh, no," said Jessaline. "I'm doing Linguistics. Or at least I was."

"Was?"

"I'm changing to Hospitality." Jessaline hadn't quite done this, not formally, not yet. She would, of course she would, but the Admin block was very near the Math building where her parents worked. They might see her; they might come out. They'd want to know why she was going to Admin.

And Clara kept wanting to know why she *hadn't* gone. "Have you gone to Admin yet?" she asked Jessaline every evening. "Have you filled in those forms?"

"Hospitality?" Clara's mum looked vague. "What is that, exactly?"

"I want to *cook*," said Jessaline, and the moment she mentioned the word, her gawky face was transformed. "I love cooking," she said simply.

Rose smiled at her. Behind the girl's shoulder she could see a pretty, homey room with pale blue walls and gay striped curtains and carpeting on the floor. "Is Clara's room like yours?" she asked.

"Pretty much," said Jessaline. "Except her walls are yellow."

"Does she have carpeting on the floor, like you?"

"Of course," said Jessaline. "Everyone has. But Mrs. Lee, here I am, a future Hospitality student, and I'm being inhospitable. Won't you come in? Have some tea? And I've got these macaroons I made last night."

Rose looked round the room. "You have a kitchen, too?"

"No," said Jessaline, smiling. "But I *will* have a kitchen, some day."

"You mean she was *here*?" Clara peered around her room as if she feared her mother might still be here, concealed behind the curtains or the wardrobe door. "She was in my room?" God, she sounded like Father Bear from Goldilocks. She sounded like *Dad*.

"No, no," said Jessaline quickly. "She was in my room; I asked her in for some tea."

Great, Clara thought. "You didn't tell her about Lonnie, did you?"

"'Course not," said Jessaline, but Clara saw the glint of uneasiness in her friend's soft brown eyes.

"You did, I bet." Jessaline was such a ... blabbermouth. She'd have let something slip, for sure.

"We talked about her library, where she works, and recipes and stuff, that's all. And, and carpets. She wanted to know if you had a carpet in your room. Or if it was bare—"

"She's got a thing about that," said Clara. "She hates wooden floors. It's almost like," Clara's voice softened, "almost like she's frightened of them."

"I could see. She was so glad you had a carpet. And Clara—"

"Yeah?"

"She was just passing by. She said to tell you that. She hadn't come to check up on you, like my folks do."

"Huh!" sad Clara. "She can't 'pass by.' This place is miles from anywhere she goes."

"I thought she was lovely," said Jessaline in a small, soft voice.

"It's all right for *you* to say so." She glared at Jessaline. "Have you been to Admin yet? To change your course?"

"Not yet. But I'm going soon."

"Soon? You've been saying that for weeks. How soon is soon?"

"It's, it's—Monday." Jessaline held out a big plastic lunch box Clara recognized from home. "She brought you these. Homemade spring rolls."

"Oh, trust *her*," said Clara crossly, but as she lifted the lid from the box and the delicious, familiar scent assailed her, tears pricked at her eyes.

33 LONNIE CLEANS HIS ROOM

Clara was coming to visit, and Lonnie knew his room looked like a mess. Messes could be cleaned up, and Lonnie had nothing against housework, because hadn't Emily Brontë done it? Hadn't she peeled potatoes for Tabby, the vicarage's old housekeeper, hadn't she washed dishes, swept and polished, mopped and scoured? And she'd even seemed to like it.

Lonnie found he liked it, too. It was great the way you found things: his green corduroy shirt beneath the desk, the pen his mum had given him that he thought he'd lost forever, and the very first note Clara had ever written to him: *"Meet you in the caf at four. Love, Clara."* A very plain, short note, businesslike even, yet somehow Lonnie spent twenty minutes on it, running the tip of his finger along the firm strokes of Clara's handwriting, smiling at the way she'd written "Love" when she could so easily have written "See ya" or nothing at all.

When you were doing housework, time seemed to speed up in the strangest fashion. As Lonnie folded Clara's note into his wallet, he saw it was half past ten. Quickly, he gathered up his scattered clothes and bundled them into the wardrobe, stacked empty pizza boxes and old newspapers into a pile beside his desk, and then began to tackle the window, which was so smeared and streaky that it let very little light into the room and you couldn't see outside. Briskly, Lonnie set to work, but when he stepped back to look at the results, he saw the smears had simply turned into circles and squares. The same mysterious thing had happened when he mopped the floor.

He had to face it; he didn't know how to clean. There was some kind of art to it, obviously, and it was one he hadn't learned. Time was really running late now; it was almost half past eleven, and Clara was coming at two. The window had to be done all over, and there were still the walls to be cleaned, and those strange sooty fingermarks around the electric switches and the wardrobe handles and the edges of the door.

Who knew how to clean?

Lonnie ran downstairs to the telephone and dialed the number of his home. It rang and rang. Of course it did. In the middle of a Wednesday his mum would be at work, and Lonnie was about to put the receiver down when a gruff, impatient voice came out of it. "Yes?"

Lily.

"How come you're home?" demanded Lonnie. "Have you started bunking off school?"

"No, I haven't!" barked Lily. "It's Curriculum Day. And *you* should talk—you were hardly ever *there*."

"But I wasn't any good at it," said Lonnie. "Not like you." His voice turned wheedling. "Hey, Lil? Hey, can you give us a hand?"

Lily sighed. She'd know that sentence anywhere. She'd heard it when she was six and he'd wanted her to hold the flashlight while he took the screws out from cranky Mrs. Grimble's mailbox; when she was eleven and he wanted her help to write a love letter—and Lily had no doubt, no doubt whatsoever, that she'd hear it when she was eighty and he was eighty-five. She didn't say yes right away though—she knew when she had the advantage. Instead she asked him, "Have you made up with Pop yet?"

"I don't know."

"What do you mean, you don't know?"

"I left him that message, didn't I?"

"A message about an old dog that's been dead for years! What good could that do?"

"It was a message," said Lonnie sulkily. "Now it's *his* turn."

Lily sighed. At this rate, Nan's party wasn't even going to get off the ground.

"Are you coming over to help?" pleaded Lonnie.

"With what?"

"Just a little spot of cleaning. Come on, Lil."

"You're a loser, Lonnie." All the same, if she went over there and gave him a hand, perhaps she could get him to make up properly with Pop, and it was ages since she'd seen Lonnie. It was eight whole months! A little bit of summer, a whole autumn, and winter …

"So are you coming?"

"I suppose so."

"You're a star!"

She'd meant to be nice to him, but when she walked into his room and her shoes stuck to the floor, all she could find to say was, "Yuk!" and then, looking around her, "You need garbage bags."

"Garbage bags?"

"Big black square things made of plastic. You get them at the supermarket."

"I know that. I'm a part-time shelf stacker, remember? I meant, what *for?*"

"All this *mess!*" roared Lily, sweeping her arms out wide. "You know where a store is?"

"Sure I do."

"Then go get some garbage bags. And —" she peered at the sticky, smudgy window, "—what are you using to clean?"

"That." Lonnie pointed to the bucket.

"Just water?"

"Yeah."

Lily sighed. "Get some window cleaner, okay. And—" she looked down at the floor and made a small grimace of disgust, "—floor cleaner, too."

"Right!"

The room looked almost wonderful when they'd finished. The window shone, and through it you could see a small green garden Lonnie hadn't even known was there, with a tiny pond and a wooden bench; and the murky floor, which he'd always thought was gray, turned out to have a cheerful pattern of blue and yellow squares. The dustbin had been emptied and the pile of old newspapers and pizza boxes gone to their final resting place in Mrs. Rasmussen's recycling bin.

Lily was exhausted. Even the journey over had taken her an hour.

Lonnie gazed round the shining room. "How come you know how to do all that?"

Lily smiled grimly. "I'm the sensible one in the family, remember?"

"Emily Brontë would have approved of you."

"What?"

"Emily Brontë was this nineteenth-century novelist ..." Lonnie paused uncertainly, aware of a kind of fury gathering on his sister's face.

"I know that!" she bellowed. "I know who Emily Brontë is. I meant, why would she have approved of me?"

"She did housework," explained Lonnie.

"Put her hand to the plow, eh?"

Lonnie flushed. "Putting your hand to the plow" was one of Pop's expressions.

The fury on Lily's face subsided to plain grievance. "Of course I know who Emily Brontë is! I've read *Wuthering Heights*! And *Jane Eyre*—and yes, I know Charlotte wrote that one! Just because I'm good at math and science doesn't mean I'm pig ig, ignum, ig ..." Some kind of distress Lily couldn't quite identify was making it difficult for her to form the word.

"Pig ignorant," Lonnie supplied helpfully.

"Shut up!" She was back to furious now, feelings welling up inside her that she hardly knew she had. How come Lonnie got everyone's attention? How come he could muck around at school and the university, keep stuffing up, and yet have a room of his own? Do what he liked? Have a life? How come he'd escaped, leaving her to do the shopping and peel carrots and remember to pay the bills? How come he had a girlfriend, while Daniel Steadman hadn't even noticed her?

"You think I'm useless, don't you?" Lonnie said suddenly.

Of course she'd thought it, many, many times. She'd been thinking it right now. Only—she didn't really mean it, at least, not in the way she could tell Lonnie meant it, in a way that was deeply serious, that meant he was good for nothing at all. "No!" she shouted.

"I'm sorry," he said simply. "I'm sorry I *act* useless."

Lily could hardly believe it. He'd never said "Sorry" in his life. Not to her, anyway, not … meaning it. Standing there in the middle of the small clean room, she thought he looked different.

"I'm sorry, too," she muttered.

A knock sounded on the door.

"Come in," said Lonnie. The door opened, and a slight dark girl carrying a big white cake box walked straight in. Lily guessed at once that this was Clara, for the girl's eyes were fixed so firmly on Lonnie that she didn't even notice there was another person in the room.

Lily's eyes moved from one to the other. "Oh," she whispered, because anyone could see that this was *serious*, and for a moment anyway her brother seemed grown-up to her. And she felt the same little pang she'd felt in this very room on the day she'd found that small piece of paper with Clara's name scribbled over and over. A pang of envy and distress—would anyone, forget about Danny Steadman, *anyone* ever gaze at her the way Lonnie was gazing at Clara? Of course they wouldn't—not when she looked like Pop, and smelled of dishwater, and was sensible and the kind of person whose dad ran off before she was even born, who couldn't even wait to see what she looked like and had never bothered since …

"Well, I'll go now," she said gruffly.

Lonnie turned, surprised. It was obvious he'd forgotten all about her.

"Lily? Um, sorry."

And a person people felt they had to keep saying "Sorry" to, thought Lily.

"Lily, this is Clara. And Clara, this is my sister, Lily." Lonnie was beaming. "Clara's, er …"

The night before Lonnie had lain awake and worked out numbers: he had his part-time job and some financial aid. If he did well in his exams, he might get a scholarship. Clara had a scholarship and part-time tutoring; they could manage. Perhaps Clara too had lain awake last night, because Lonnie knew when he looked into her eyes that she'd come to the same conclusions he had. He didn't even have to ask. "Clara's my girlfriend," he told Lily. "We—" a sudden perfect certainty rushed upon him. Lonnie had never felt so sure. "We're engaged."

"She's beautiful," Lily told her mum. "And nice, you know? Only—"

All the way home on the train Lily had been worrying about this: how when Pop heard Lonnie was engaged to a Chinese girl, he'd go ballistic. Pop was prehistoric in that way: he knew all these awful racist jokes, and he told them, too, without even noticing that nobody else was laughing. He'd travel miles on jolting trains—with a toothache—to find some awful old Aussie dentist who was just like him, because he wouldn't trust a "New Australian" to fix his teeth. The very best you could say about Pop was that he was in severe bad taste.

"Only?" Her mother's voice interrupted Lily's painful reverie.

"What?"

"You said, 'She's beautiful, and nice, only—' Only what?"

"Oh, nothing."

"I can't wait to meet her at the party. They are coming, aren't they?"

"Yes, they are," said Lily dismally. Lonnie had told her this as she was leaving, as they stood together on the front step of 5 Firth Street, Lily clutching the white box in which Clara had placed two slices of cherry cake made by someone called Jessaline. They'd asked her to stay, but Lily had pretended she had an urgent school assignment; these days she felt awkward with people in love.

"You're *both* coming?" she'd asked, and Lonnie had nodded cheerfully.

"But Pop—"

"Oh," Lonnie had tossed his long front lock back from his forehead. "I reckon he'll come round. I'm still doing my course, aren't I?"

"I didn't mean that. I meant—" Couldn't he figure *anything* out? He'd heard Pop's jokes. That one about the Chinese man and the Japanese man and the Arab—yuk! And then she saw the tiny nervous flicker in his eyes and thought he might have figured it out, this time. "Look, I think," she'd begun, but he waved her words aside.

"It'll be all right," he'd said.

"You wish."

"Pop's going to hate her," Lily said now to Mum.

"Why should he?"

"She's Chinese," muttered Lily.

"So?"

Her mother didn't get it. Mum and Lonnie had quite a bit in common; they were like a pair of half-blind sailors on a leaky old ship who couldn't look out and see the rocks ahead.

"Oh, come on, Mum. Pop's such an old racist. When he finds out Lonnie's engaged to a Chinese girl, he's going to explode! He'll throw them out!"

"Of course he won't," her mother said calmly. "Your pop's all talk."

"His talk is *enough*. What if he tells one of his awful jokes?"

"He won't."

"How can you tell?"

"I just know. Having Clara in the family will be good for him."

Lily gave up. She stomped off to her room, where she couldn't get to sleep, where she kept on seeing Clara and Lonnie coming through the gate of her grandparents' cottage, and—Lily's vision of Nan's party darkened, the flowers wilted, streamers fell, the fairy lights went out in the trees. And she'd wanted so much one lovely, perfect day ...

When Mum had gone to bed, Lily tiptoed from her room and crept softly down the hall toward the telephone. She lifted the receiver and laid the thin handkerchief she'd taken from her drawer across its mouthpiece—as she'd seen kidnappers do in movies—then dialed the familiar number, crossing her fingers that Pop would be the one to answer the phone. She knew he often stayed up late, watching boring old war documentaries that sent Nan hastily off to bed.

The phone rang. "Yeah?"

It was him, and for a moment, Lily faltered. Then she thought of how Nan's party must be perfect, took a steadying breath, and in a low voice spoke into the telephone. "Sir, I'm doing a survey, on behalf of the, um, the Association for Racial Harmony."

"Racial what?"

"Harmony."

"What's that? Something to do with music?"

"No, it's, um, about different cultures."

Disguised voice, thought Stan, that old trick of the hanky over the phone, and for a moment he thought the voice might be Lonnie's because of how Lonnie had been up here only the other day.

"Been *here!*" Stan had shouted, when May had given him the news. "Here? When I told him to keep away, when I told him he was no grandson of mine?"

"He came to make up with you, I think," said May. "He left you a message."

"What message?"

"He said to tell you he was sorry about old Ratbag."

Ratbag! Stan had gone quite silent. His old pal, Ratbag. Lonnie had remembered him! Lonnie had been no more than a pup himself when the old dog had died. Not a day passed that Stan didn't think of Ratbag, imagining him—idiotically, he knew—up there in the sky somewhere looking down at them, wagging his tail. And Lonnie had remembered him, when everyone else except Stan had put him out of mind! Lonnie! Stan had found himself struggling against a dangerous softening of the heart ...

"I want Lonnie to come to this party," May had said, her blue eyes regarding him steadily, almost sternly.

"Didn't say he couldn't, did I?" Stan had retorted, and May had turned away and walked out from the room. "Tell him he can come."

Stan had called after her, and her voice floated back to him from the hall. "I *did* tell him. But you have to tell him, too."

He hadn't, yet.

"Sir? Sir, are you still there?" This muffled voice on the telephone wasn't Lonnie; he realized that the minute he heard that familiar little catch between the words. It was Lil. When she was nervous, there was always that catch in Lily's voice.

"Yeah," he said.

"So would you be interested in taking part in our survey? In the cause of ... of peace?"

"Peace, eh? Okay."

"We're targeting gentleman over seventy. Would you be in that age group, sir?"

"Bet your life I am."

"All right, um—did you fight in the war, sir? The Second World War, I mean."

"No, I had flat f— I had a medical condition."

A muffled snort sounded over the line.

"Sir, I hope you don't mind me asking this next question?"

"Spit it out!"

"Sir, do you hate the Japanese?"

"No!"

"Or other ethnic groups, sir?"

"No!"

Lily's voice was now quite clear. In her enthusiasm she must have let the hanky slip; Stan imagined it fluttering, unnoticed, to the floor. He pictured the gloomy hallway she stood in: the ancient flaking paper on the walls, the musty odor—he was sure—of rising dampness. There was a hole in the skirting board where May swore she'd once seen a tiny pair of twitching whiskers and brilliant, darting eyes. He hated that house. How could they live there? Geez, he'd like to burn it down.

"Sir?"

"Yeah?"

"Sir, my next question is, er ..."

"Get it off your chest!"

"Sir, what would you do if a grandchild of yours was planning to get married to, um, someone of another race?"

"I'd pin her ears back!" roared Stan. "If any granddaughter of mine tried marrying *anyone*, when she's only sixteen and hasn't finished school!"

Lily dropped the phone.

"Who was that?" asked May, as a grinning Stan came loping back into the living room.

"Association for Racial Harmony."

"What on earth did they want with you?"

"Survey," chuckled Stan.

"What were they surveying?"

Stan shrugged. "Dunno."

He did, though. Or at least he had an inkling.

The next afternoon the inkling was more definite. He was out in the back weeding around the silver beets when May came rushing from the house. "Guess what?" she cried. Her face was glowing.

He could have guessed and got it right, only he didn't want to spoil her surprise.

"You tell me."

"Lonnie and Clara have got engaged!"

Clara, eh? Stan remembered the Chinese woman he'd met in the park whose daughter's name was Clara. He'd had a sort of feeling, even at the time. "Coincidences do happen," he said aloud, and May gave him a puzzled glance.

"You mean it's a coincidence Lonnie's got engaged just when we were having our party?"

Stan smiled and put his arm about her shoulders. "That too," he said.

35 MORE RESTLESS NIGHTS

It was happening again: that sharp little niggle that would wake Stan two hours after he'd fallen asleep and keep him lying there staring at the ceiling while the niggling went on and on—like he was a table, Stan thought, and some cranky little kid was kicking at one of his legs. What was bothering him? Last time it had been the way he couldn't remember the color of Mum's eyes; he'd sorted that one out, and it had made no difference so perhaps it hadn't been the problem in the first place? What was the problem then? Stan pushed the covers back and got out of bed; there was no way he'd get back to sleep.

"You all right, love?" May murmured sleepily.

"Just off to get a drink of milk," Stan reassured her.

As he approached the fridge, Lonnie's name stared at him from the door, and the address, and his telephone number too, and Stan could almost swear the figures in that number had been made larger, as if to give a gentle hint. Well, he wasn't phoning him!

He poured the milk into a tumbler, gulped it down quickly, returned the carton to the fridge—and saw the message all over again: Lonnie: 5 Firth Street, Toongabbie. Telephone 98614532. He'd rip it down except for the upset that would cause May. She kept on nagging, reminding him that Lonnie hadn't dropped out of this latest course of his, that he was working, and that it was he, Stan, who'd lost his block back there last summer.

"And I had reason to," Stan retorted, digging in his heels.

And yet, Ratbag! He couldn't get over how Lonnie had remembered the old dog and remembered, too, because that seemed to be the gist of the message, how upset Stan had been.

Stan downed the milk and rinsed the glass under the faucet. Perhaps it wouldn't hurt to—to what? Make it up? *Apologize?* The very word embarrassed him; a man had his pride, didn't he? And whatever May said, he'd had good reasons for writing Lonnie off last summer.

Writing him off—the phrase triggered a sudden image of that girl he'd encountered on the train, the beggar girl in black. Stan saw her now with enormous clarity: the thin, dusty clothes; the small mound of her stomach; the unwashed hair and grubby fingernails; the frightening sound of her voice. He pictured her sodden cardboard hideaway again, imagined her lying in it at the dead of night listening to footsteps passing on the pavement, heart beating fast, holding her breath when the footsteps stopped. Perhaps it was the thought of her, half forgotten, that kept waking him up at night. "Shouldn't be allowed," he muttered.

Something should be done.

Like what? What could be done? He was old and out of touch these days; he didn't know the city as he had years back when he was young and on the force. He didn't know where such a girl might go to get help, proper help, not people who'd push her around. He didn't know whom she should see, and it made him feel useless, this being out of touch.

Who would know, then?

Marigold.

Stan padded down the hall toward the telephone.

• • •

Marigold struggled up from sleep, saw the time on the bedside clock: 2:30—the time for very bad news. *"Lonnie?"* she whispered, picking up the phone.

"Lonnie?" Stan was outraged. "It's *me.*"

Dad. Marigold drew in a quick, frightened breath. If Dad was calling at this hour, then something must have happened to Mum. "Mum?"

"It's *me*, I said!" roared Stan. "How could you think I was your mother?"

"I *know* it's you!" Marigold roared back. "I meant—is something wrong with Mum?"

"Why should there be? She's dead to the world—snoring her head off back there in bed. Like I would be, too, if it wasn't for this girl."

Marigold froze. Girl? Was he talking about Clara?

"What girl?" she asked.

"This kid I saw on the train. Beggar kid—pregnant, deaf and dumb, walking up and down the carriage." Stan cleared his throat. "Hardly older than Lil."

Marigold listened in astonishment as her tough old dad, at two thirty in the morning, when he'd normally be sound asleep, went on about this girl in black. "Thought you might know what to do," he finished gruffly.

Marigold gave him names and addresses, phone numbers. "But no matter what you do, Dad, there are kids who fall right through the cracks."

Stan hung up the phone. "Fall through the cracks." What an expression! His mum would have hated it. It was almost as bad as "written him off."

• • •

Marigold sank down onto the sofa. Lily appeared in the doorway, rubbing her fists in her eyes. "Who was that?"

"Your pop."

"What did he ring about? Nan's all right, isn't she?"

"Of course."

"So?"

"You're not going to believe this."

Lily tightened her lips. "Try me."

"Your tough old pop is worried about this young girl he has seen begging on the train. Sixteen, pregnant, deaf and dumb, dressed all in black—"

"I've seen that girl," said Lily, "lots of times. Lonnie has, too."

A couple of years back Lily would have scorned that girl in black—a druggie, she'd have thought, a loser. Because how else could you get like that? Now, at sixteen, Lily had worked out that anything could happen to anybody if there was no one around to catch you when you fell.

"I've seen her lots," she repeated. She flung herself down on the sofa and leaned her head against her mother's shoulder.

"Have you?"

"She's scary." Lily paused. "When you said it was Pop, I thought it might be he'd found out."

"Found out what?"

"Found out about Clara being Chinese."

"Lily, I'm sure it won't be like that."

"Yes it will!" Lily stared down at her toes. They were short and stubby, like Pop's. Somewhere in *Bestie* there'd be a feature on how to make your toes look long and slender even if they weren't. But she'd finished with all that, finished with crushes and all that girlish stuff, finished with Daniel

Steadman—her toes would stay as they were. All she cared about now was Nan's party. "I know exactly what's going to happen," she told her mum. "Lonnie will show up with Clara, and the moment Pop sees her, he'll start going on, and Clara will get upset, like, who *wouldn't?*" Lily put her hands up to her eyes, as if she could actually see these awful things happening—"and Lonnie will get mad, and he and Pop will have a big fight again, and then, then Clara will want to go home, and Nan's party will be ruined!"

"No, no," soothed Marigold.

"Yes! And Mum," Lily threw her arms out wide, despairingly, "it could have been this brilliant, perfect day!"

"Lily, it will be."

"No, it *can't* be."

"Why not?"

"We're too ... dysfunctional."

"Show me a family that isn't." Marigold actually chuckled, infuriating Lily.

"Mum! Can't you take things seriously?"

Before their eyes this time, a very small mouse skidded from behind the TV, gazed at them boldly for a second, and then darted out through the door.

Lily waved a hand after his vanishing tail. "See! We've even got rats in the family room!"

"I think it was a mouse."

"Makes no difference." Lily made a another wide, sweeping gesture, encompassing their tatty rug, which never got clean no matter which shampoo you used; the battered furniture, second-hand when Mum had first been married; those scary leak stains on the ceiling (how did you fix a *roof*?). Lily had been brought up to believe that material things weren't important, and she still believed this, except—other people didn't. Tracy Gilman's eyes would go big and round if she ever got inside this house.

And Daniel Steadman? Lily tossed her head. What Daniel Steadman might think didn't matter now. Not only had she given up on him, but Daniel seemed to have vanished from school, and Lily wasn't vain enough to think he'd disappeared because of her. No, he'd simply left, as people do. Gone to another school, perhaps—people changed schools all the time. Someone would know: kids in his year who took the same classes, Mr. Corcoran, even Tracy Gilman. But she wasn't asking anyone; Daniel Steadman had been a mistake, and a humiliation. There were other things to do in life; there was … for a frightening moment Lily couldn't think of anything. She'd concentrate on her schoolwork then, she decided. She'd … she'd devote herself to science; she was good at physics and chemistry. She'd be strong and stern and famous, like … like Madame Curie. Yes! That was it! She'd be the Madame Curie of the twenty-first century!

"Lily?"

Mum was smiling at her.

"Yeah?"

"Lily, I know I promised you I wouldn't bring any more lame ducks home—"

"Mum!"

"But this one, she's special."

"You always say that." Lily sat up straight and folded her arms sternly.

"Honestly, this one is. And it's only for a weekend, darling."

"What weekend?"

"This coming one."

Something like the beginning of a smile quivered at the corners of Lily's lips. A moment ago she'd have thought things couldn't get worse. Now it seemed they could, and, well, you had to look on the funny side. "Good one, Mum," she said.

"Good one?"

"The party's next weekend."

"Ah." Marigold frowned, and then she brightened. "I'm sure Nan won't mind an extra guest. In fact, she'd probably love one. Don't you think?"

Lily nodded.

"And I'm sure Mrs. Nightingale will fit in wonderfully," Marigold went on merrily.

"Yeah," agreed Lily. "In *our* family, I bet she will."

36 FIVE FIRTH STREET, TOONGABBIE

Armed with Marigold's list of helpful names and agencies, Stan traveled into the city to look for the girl in black. He rode up and down on the trains all morning: Penrith to Blacktown, Blacktown to Parramatta, into Strathfield and the city, where he grabbed a sandwich at Wynyard and then traveled out again. At each station he went to the doors and leaned out, scanning the platforms, getting in people's way. "Watch out, Pop!" a young voice shouted, and Stan looked around sharply because for a moment he'd thought it might be Lon, but of course it wasn't, only some kid who thought it was fine to call any bloke over forty "Pop." "Get stuffed," retorted Stan, and the kid gave him the finger. Stan gave it to him back. No way he was putting up with cheek.

At half past three, slowing into a suburb west of Parramatta and with still no sign of the girl, Stan decided to call it a day. Where was he now? What station was this? The sign slid by the window: Toongabbie, read Stan, and all at once he was on his feet and headed for the door.

It wouldn't hurt, he told himself, since he was passing this way anyway, to take a gander at the place, to see this dump where Lonnie lived. Down the ramp, out into the street—

"Firth Street?" he asked the bloke at the gate.

"Two blocks down, turn right at the service station. Can't miss it."

"Thanks, mate."

The house surprised him. He knew from May and Marigold that it wasn't a shack; all the same he'd expected some kind of hovel, seedy and damp, the garden full of weeds and other rubbish—a bit like Marigold's home, only with more people in it. He hadn't bargained for fresh paint on the doors and windowsills and the downspouts in place.

"Not bad," he thought, studying Mrs. Rasmussen's well-kept front garden from the opposite side of the street. Five minutes passed, and he was still standing there, shifting from foot to foot, unable to work out exactly why he was here.

It was May's fault, of course; her fault for sticking that notice up on the fridge, lodging Lonnie's address so firmly in his brain, that when he saw the word *Toongabbie*, he'd walked out onto the platform as if this had been his destination all along.

Programmed, like a robot—but now he was here on the spot. He might as well have a go at seeing Lonnie. Not to apologize, mind you—simply have a bit of a chat.

What could he say to him? Stan looked up and down the street, as if the answer might lie there. He saw old houses, some neat and tidy like 5 Firth Street, some renovated, others merely old. There'd be old people living here, and Stan wished one of them was outside in their front yard so he could wander up and have the sort of natter he often had at bus stops and railway stations with people of his age, about kids and grandkids, what to do …

He gazed at the bright blue door of Lonnie's boarding house. Should he go over there? It was almost four thirty, the tail end of the afternoon, and Lonnie would most probably be out, though you couldn't really tell because uni students kept all kinds of hours and he might be in.

Okay—so what he'd do, Stan decided, if Lonnie *was* home, was to act quite natural, as if his outburst on that afternoon last summer and that silly business with the ax, had never actually occurred.

He stepped out from the sidewalk and then, in the middle of the road, stopped dead. What if Lonnie's girlfriend was in there? And what if Lonnie had told her about that business with the ax? If he'd done that, and you could bet he had because Lon was never one to hide his troubles, then the girlfriend—Clara—probably thought he was some kind of monster. She'd shriek when she caught sight of him.

"Get off the bloody road, Pop!" Stan jerked his head around and found a big red utility truck almost on top of him, a pop-eyed, outraged young face glaring from the driver's window.

"'Sir', to you! I'm no pop of yours, ya little bugger! Have some respect, why don't you!"

He got the finger again. The truck roared off. In the front room of 5 Firth Street he glimpsed a curtain twitch—someone had been watching him!

It could even be the girlfriend.

Stan took to his heels.

Up in the hills May walked slowly around her garden. The lawn, thanks to winter rain and Stan's new mower, was soft as velvet underfoot; and if there was no frost this week, those feathery clusters of buds on the wisteria might just bloom early and become, by the weekend of the party, long mauve sprays of flowers. The last two days had been mild and sunny, there was brightness in the air, and the foggy dew had melted away by midmorning, the blue folds of the mountains etched clear and sharp against a cloudless sky. At midday you could feel a genuine warmth to the sun, where it fell on your face and arms.

May hoped for two such days for the party weekend: "Two perfect, cloudless days," she said to Sef. "That's what we need." Two perfect, cloudless days when Stan and Lonnie would make up and Clara be welcomed into the family. May drew in a deep, excited breath. Only a few more days to go! A wave of happiness washed over her; she felt like dancing! She had a sudden bright memory of Sef and herself dancing in the hall of the children's home: round and round they went, hair flying, skirts billowing—Christmas, it must have been—faster and faster, the sunlit windows flying past like dreams ...

One of the good things about getting old was how these happy moments from the past returned to you: the scents and sounds and colors, the *feel* of everything. In the bright green garden May held out her arms. "Let's dance!" she said to Sef, and, slowly, because after all Sef would be seventy-eight her next birthday, slowly but gracefully, back straight, head held high, May began to dance across Stan's lawn.

Rattled by his visit to Firth Street, Stan lost his way in the back streets of Toongabbie and wandered for a full half hour. Then at the station he got confused and went to the city side. He didn't even notice the train he boarded there was going in the wrong direction until it stopped at Strathfield, and there he stood on the platform, lost in a daze.

He should have left a note for Lonnie. "Thanks for remembering Ratbag!" or something of that kind, enough to show there were no hard feelings anymore. Five Firth Street was a boarding house; there'd have been a spot where you could leave mail—"Should have walked right in," mumbled Stan. "Should have."

Someone tapped him on the shoulder. Stan turned and saw the Chinese lady he'd met in the park the month before, the one with the daughter named Clara. She was breathless, beaming at him. "Saw you," she gasped. "Saw you, and *ran*."

"Ran?"

"I was over there—" she waved toward the opposite platform. "And I wanted so much to thank you—"

"Thank me?"

"Remember how I wanted to go and see my daughter's place, and you said I had a right?"

"And you went, eh?"

She nodded.

Braver than he was, then.

"She wasn't in. But I saw her friend next door, and she said her room was just like Clara's, so now I can picture her, you know? And if it wasn't for you, I don't think I'd have gone! I'm going to go again! I'm going to call her and—you know what? I think she's got a boyfriend!"

"Boyfriend? Look, is his name—"

A train thundered into the station on the opposite side of the tracks, drowning out his words. The Chinese lady whirled round. "There's my train!"

"Lonnie?" finished Stan. "Is your daughter's boyfriend named Lonnie?"

She didn't hear him; she was running for the stairs. His own train slid to a stop beside the platform. It was dark already, getting late up at Katoomba, May would soon start to worry. Stan stepped on board.

• • •

"My grandfather?" Lonnie stared at Mrs. Rasmussen, appalled. She'd caught him the moment he came through the front door, her face alight with news. "Pop's been here?" Lonnie glanced nervously round the hallway, into shadowy corners he'd barely noticed before. *"Here?"* he said again.

Mrs. Rasmussen nodded happily. Lonnie could see she thought this was something to be glad about. She didn't understand the complications of his family, like how everyone was always fighting and misunderstanding one another and how he didn't know why Pop had come. Was it to make up from their quarrel finally? Or to bawl him out again?

"What did he say?" he asked.

Mrs. Rasmussen shrugged. "Ah, nothing."

"Nothing?" That didn't sound like Pop. Pop was like Lily; when they got worked up, they went on and on and on.

"He didn't come inside," explained Mrs. Rasmussen.

"He didn't?"

She shook her head, pointing toward the sidewalk on the other side of the road. "He stood there," she said, "and looked toward this house for a very long time, as if he wished to come in. He even crossed the road, halfway, only I think he was—"

"What?"

"Shy." Mrs. Rasmussen didn't mention how the poor old man had almost been run down. The truck had missed him after all, so why make a fuss?

Shy? Pop? Lonnie couldn't imagine that. How could someone like Pop be shy? Perhaps Mrs. Rasmussen had got the wrong grandpa; there were a lot of old people in this neighborhood.

"What was he wearing?" Lonnie knew, on a cold day

like this, Pop would have been wearing his old green jacket and the brown felt hat he and Lily had often giggled about, because surely it was left over from the days when Pop had been a cop.

"A green jacket," replied Mrs. Rasmussen promptly. "And a funny hat—like detectives wear on TV. In old movies. You know?"

"Yeah," mumbled Lonnie. "That was him." That's all right, thought Lonnie. All right.

37 HOPES AND DREAMS

Only it wasn't right. Lonnie couldn't get to sleep that night from wondering and worrying, thrashing about beneath the covers, wrenching his pillow this way and that, and trying to find a comfortable place for his head, which was buzzing with thoughts of Pop's visit and Nan's party, now only a few short days away. Why had Pop come here?

"Did he look angry?" he'd asked Mrs. Rasmussen, but she could only repeat that she thought his pop had looked shy. Lonnie twisted and turned, twitched at his pillow, kicked the covers down and dragged them up, until, in the early hours, he thought he saw Emily Brontë in her long brown gown standing by his bed.

"Stop it," she said sharply. Was he dreaming? The stuff of her brown gown looked so real he felt he could reach out and touch it ...

"Stop what?" he whispered, but he couldn't hear her answer, which he thought might be important, because his eyes were growing heavy and she was misting over—"Wait," he whispered, "wait." She didn't wait, and it didn't matter because, quite suddenly, Lonnie was sound asleep.

On the other side of the city, in her small room at the top of Mercer Hall, Clara too was wide awake. She lay in the dark and pictured her mother setting out to visit her the week before. Even though, on certain clear days, you could see the tower of Mercer Hall from the front porch of Clara's old home, by public transport her mother's journey would have taken a long, long time. She pictured Mum closing the front door carefully behind her, walking down the path and through the gate, around the corner, on down Harkness Street toward the station. She saw her sitting on the train and then standing waiting at the cold bus stop on Eddy Avenue, the box of spring rolls lying in the bottom of her bag. She imagined her walking across the windy campus, tall buildings all around her, so that Mum would have seemed very small.

Then Clara heard her own voice telling Mum how she shouldn't put up with Dad's sulks and bossiness. "You're too soft on him, Mum! Stand up for yourself!" she heard herself scolding, and then, like a weird stranger walking through a door, an odd idea stole into Clara's mind. It was this: how toward her mother, alone of everyone else on earth, Clara was … a bit of a bully, just like Dad.

Clara's Mum and Dad both dreamed of her that night. "My mum makes the *best* spring rolls!" Clara told Jessaline in Rose's dream; in Charlie's dream, Clara was only little and he was showing her around his office, when suddenly she caught his hand, smiled up at him, and whispered, "You're my favorite dad in the whole *world!*"

Jessaline dreamed of the restaurant she'd have one day: she saw its walled courtyard and pink flagstones and the white wooden tables and chairs. *"Chez Jessaline,"* she murmured.

Jessaline's mum woke suddenly and nudged Jessaline's dad. "Victor!" she said.

"What?" replied Jessaline's dad sleepily.

"Victor, do you think our Jessaline is happy doing Linguistics?"

"Happy?" mumbled Jessaline's dad sleepily "Did you say 'happy'? What's that got to do with it?"

Jessaline's mum spoke as if she'd had a revelation. "A lot, I think!" she said.

Once—such a short time back—Lily had longed to dream of Daniel Steadman, even to the point of writing out his name and sliding it beneath her pillow. Now she didn't want to dream of him; she wanted to dream of Madame Curie instead, strong and imposing in her white lab coat. And wouldn't you know it! Because she didn't want to dream of Daniel, for the very first time she did. It was the most peculiar dream: he was wearing pajamas, he stood in a gateway holding a rolled-up newspaper in his hand. "Oh, *hi!*" he said, smiling.

Daniel dreamed of the beautiful voice again.

Marigold dreamed that Lonnie walked into the house carrying the biggest pumpkin she'd ever seen. "Hi, Mum!" he greeted her. "I'm engaged. And here's Clara!"

"Where?" asked Marigold, and then Lonnie touched the pumpkin, and it burst open and a tiny slender girl stood there.

When Stan reached home after his visit to Firth Street, he found May at the kitchen table making place cards for the party. Yesterday she'd been making invitations. "You send an invite yet to Lon and Clara?" he asked gruffly.

May smiled and patted a small stack of envelopes on the corner of the table. "Sending them tomorrow," she said. "That's Lonnie's on the top. I didn't seal the envelope just in case." She took out the card.

Stan plucked it from her fingers and grabbed a pen. He opened the card and wrote, "Thanks for remembering Ratbag! Looking forward to seeing you and Clara at the party." Then he passed it to May. "That do you?"

"I *knew* you'd come around!"

"Didn't know I'd been unconscious," said Stan smartly. That night he slept soundly, but May lay awake in a little daze of happiness, and when the moon began to sail across the window, its light blooming through the thin white curtains, she whispered to Sef, "I know we're going to have a perfect, cloudless day!"

Old Mrs. Nightingale dreamed she was dancing.

38 NONE OF OUR BUSINESS

It was the Saturday before the party when Clara's mum decided to call her daughter at Mercer Hall. Rose reasoned, that on a Saturday, if she called fairly early—say, at 9 a.m.— she'd have a better chance of catching Clara at home.

But it was Jessaline, on her way back from the bathroom, who heard the phone shrill out along the corridor. And when she heard it, Jessaline stood very, very still while her heart gave a big bound and then settled coldly down beneath her ribs. There were fifteen other girls with rooms on the twentieth floor, yet Jessaline was absolutely sure this call was meant for her. The morning of the day before, sneaking past the building where her parents worked, the hood of her parka drawn close about her face, Jessaline had finally found her way to Admin and filled in forms to change her course from Linguistics to Hospitality. Her hand had trembled as she filled in her name and student number, and her bottom lip was drawn in so sharply between her big front teeth that there'd still been marks there in the evening when she'd cleaned them.

The woman behind the counter at Admin had worried Jessaline. Her face had seemed familiar, as if Jessaline had met her before—not in the Admin office but somewhere else, somewhere like ... home, where her parents were always having dinner parties for their colleagues, hosting educational committees, and entertaining scholars from overseas. When she'd lived there, Jessaline had often been called on to pass around plates of appetizers and cups of coffee and tea so that all kinds of people at the university knew she was the daughter of the two Professors O'Harris.

When she'd left the Admin building, Jessaline had circled around it and hidden in a small courtyard for ten minutes before sneaking back inside: she wanted to see if the familiar-looking woman was talking on the telephone—calling Mum or Dad. She hadn't been, but that didn't make Jessaline feel any better: once the contents of that form began to circulate, it wouldn't be long before her parents came to know, and this ringing phone, so loud and insistent on the twentieth floor of Mercer Hall, could very well be them. Jessaline put her hands over her ears and hurried into her room. The phone kept ringing; she could hear it through the door.

She couldn't *bear* it. She knew her mum and dad; they were the kind of people who would keep on calling until they got an answer, and if there was no one to answer, then they would get into their car and come right over. They'd knock on the door until she opened it. "Jessaline!" they'd exclaim. "What's this we hear?" Jessaline thought of the beautiful courtyard she'd glimpsed in her dream the other night: the courtyard of *Chez Jessaline*—once again she saw the pink flagstones, the white chairs and tables, the scented jasmine climbing up the wall. Then she squared her shoulders and approached the telephone. She'd have to have it out with them sometime, so why not get it over with? "It's my life, not yours!"—that's what she'd say.

She picked up the receiver. "Hullo?"

"Is that Mercer Hall? Floor 20?" The light sweet voice was definitely not Dad, or Mum.

"Yes," said Jessaline.

"Could I speak to Clara Lee?"

• • •

"Mrs. Lee! It's you!" Jessaline was delighted. "Mrs. Lee, guess what? You know I told you I was going to change my course to Hospitality? Well, I've done it! I really have!"

"That's wonderful, Jessaline."

Why couldn't her own mum be so nice? Why couldn't her own mum, or even her dad, ever say, "That's wonderful!"?

Jessaline sighed. "You're looking for Clara, aren't you, Mrs. Lee? I'm afraid she's gone."

"Gone?" The word sent a chilly tingle creeping down Rose's spine. What did that mean?

"You mean she's left the hall? Gone to live somewhere else? Left—left the university?"

"Oh no," replied Jessaline, surprised. "Nothing like that, Mrs. Lee. She's just gone away for the weekend with her fiancé, you know? They've gone up to the mountains to visit Lonnie's grandparents. It's his grandfather's birthday. His eightieth, imagine!"

"*Fiancé?*"

"Oh!" gasped Jessaline. She'd done it again! That big mouth of hers! She'd forgotten that Clara's engagement was a secret, from her parents anyway.

"I'm going to tell them later," Clara had explained. "After the party. After I've met Lonnie's family, and things have sort of settled down."

"What things?" Jessaline had asked, but Clara hadn't told her.

"Where does he live?" Mrs. Lee was asking on the phone. How funny her voice had gone. The lightness had leaked right out of it; she sounded suddenly businesslike, almost … stern.

"Lonnie? Um, I don't know exactly. I think it's out

Toongabbie way. But they won't be there, Mrs. Lee. They'll be up at Lonnie's grandfather's place."

"That's what I meant. Where do the grandparents live?"

"Oooh," said Jessaline. "Are you going to go *there?*" She was shocked. Even *her* parents wouldn't do a thing like that. Jessaline frowned. Or would they?

"I might," replied Mrs. Lee. "Where do they live?"

How could such a nice lady suddenly turn so scary? Jessaline wondered.

"Jessaline!"

"In Katoomba," she answered hopelessly. "I don't know the exact address."

"His name? The grandfather's?"

"Stan. I don't know his last name, Mrs. Lee. Honest. Only I don't think that matters because Clara says Lonnie told her everyone in Katoomba knows his grandpa because he's such a loudmouth. He says you can ask anyone in the street for Stan, and they'll know who you mean."

"Thank you, Jessaline."

Jessaline had barely replaced the receiver when the phone shrilled out again. This time she *knew* it was her parents. She picked up the receiver and said into it: "It's my life, not yours."

"She's engaged," Rose said to Charlie.

Charlie's face tensed up into a scowl. Wrinkles sprang out of nowhere; his lips went tight and thin.

Engaged, eh? That would be the punk he'd seen her kissing in the street. Punk! Charlie relished the word, even though he wasn't sure precisely what it meant. He knew one thing, though—his daughter would choose the kind of person who'd annoy her father most, and that would be—a punk. An Australian punk. "Ah, yes," he said to Rose.

Rose rounded on him. "Is that all you can say?"

Charlie was silent.

"I'm going up there!" cried Rose.

"Up where?"

"To Katoomba, where this boy's grandparents live. Where this Stan lives."

"Stan?"

"The boy's grandfather, this *Lonnie's* grandfather. Your daughter's future grandfather-in-law—"

"Grandfather-in-law?"

"I'm going up there, to—to see!"

Rose rushed around the bedroom flinging bits and pieces into a small bag, just in case she couldn't find this grandpa's place and had to stay overnight in a hotel and begin her search again the next day. Oh, she was angry, so angry—to move out of home, that was one thing; she could understand perfectly why Clara had had to do that. And though it was hurtful, she could even understand why Clara wanted to keep her new home a secret, and her boyfriend, too. But to become engaged and not speak a word of it—Rose made an odd little hooting sound. When she'd become engaged to Charlie all those years ago, her single sadness had been that she had no mum and dad to tell.

Charlie hovered in the doorway. "Don't cry," he said, gently—for him. "Don't cry, Rose."

"I'll cry if I want to!"

Charlie's voice hardened. "Let me get this straight," he said. "You're going to Katoomba. You're going to a total stranger's place, some old chap you've never met, whose last name you don't even know, and whose address you don't know—"

"I need to," said Rose simply.

"It's none of our business, don't you understand? If she wants to get herself engaged and not tell us, if she wants to go to some old man's party, it's—"

"I'm going." Rose snapped the locks shut on her bag.

"None of our business," Charlie repeated lamely.

"Yes it is. She's our daughter."

"*Was*," said Charlie. "Was our daughter."

"Ah!" the glance Rose flung at him was withering. "No one ever stops being someone's child."

39 THE MESSAGE

"Come early on the Saturday," Nan had urged Lonnie on the telephone. "Come early, the day before the party. Then we can have the whole weekend to get to know Clara properly."

So Lonnie and Clara took the 8:30 from Strathfield, Lonnie carrying Pop's present: a set of fancy screwdrivers in a polished wooden case. And Clara carried a big bunch of flowers, a Noah's ark of flowers: two roses, two tulips, two carnations, two irises, two daffodils—two of everything.

As their train passed Lidcombe, a shadow passed over Clara's face, like a curtain drawn across a window, shutting out the light. She shivered, and the big bunch of flowers trembled on her lap in sympathy. She'd caught a glimpse of her old school, and behind it, in the very next street, was the house where she'd grown up and where her parents lived. She could just make out the tip of its red roof. Clara drew in a long, shaky breath.

"What is it?" asked Lonnie, sliding his arm around her shoulders.

"Nothing," she said, twitching away from him.

"If you're worried about Pop—"

"I'm not."

"But if you are—"

"I said I'm not."

Perhaps, thought Lonnie, he shouldn't have warned her that Pop could sound a bit prehistoric sometimes. Even sound racist, if you didn't know him—

"We can get out at Parramatta," he said. "No worries. Nan'll understand."

Clara shook her head fiercely. Lonnie squeezed her hand. "Look, if Pop—"

"I'm not worried about your pop!" she burst out. "It's *my* family! Don't you understand?"

"Your family?"

"I saw my house back there. It's, oh—Mum!" Clara covered her face with her hands.

"Your mum? Is she sick or something?"

"No! It's—I should have *told* her. I should have called her up and told her about you. I should have told her we were engaged. Like you told your mum! I should have thanked her for the spring rolls!"

Now he was really lost. "Spring rolls?"

"She came to Mercer Hall when I was out and left them for me. Because they're my very favorite. And I didn't call to thank her because I was so mad she'd been there without even telling me. And you know, I told you, how she wants to see my room, how she'd wanted to see it for months and months, and I've put her off, and—I'm a bully!" howled Clara. "That's what I am—I'm a bully just like Dad!"

"'Course you're not a bully."

"Yes I am!"

"No, you're not."

They might have gone on like this all the way to Penrith except that suddenly Clara broke off with a short, startled gasp. Lonnie looked around. The girl in black was standing right beside their seat.

She was bigger now than when Stan had encountered her, her swelling stomach pushed out against the thin stuff of her dress, and there were pools of purply shadow underneath her eyes.

Clara had never seen her—living in Mercer Hall, she hardly ever traveled on the trains, but Lonnie had come across her many, many times, and he often thought of her as he lay safe in bed at night. He'd wondered what kind of place she lived in and if there was anything that could be done. And only the night before he'd got the answer, like an inspiration.

Mum! Mum took in lame ducks, so—why not this lost girl? And there were heaps of space at home since he'd moved out. Well, more space anyway.

Clara was reading the girl's placard with big, scared eyes. Lonnie fumbled through his wallet and then the back pockets of his jeans. The girl in black began to move away.

"No, don't go!" mouthed Lonnie, reaching out to touch her arm. The touch did it: she waited while his fingers searched the pockets of his shirt.

"What are you looking for?" asked Clara.

"This bit of paper I had."

"Paper?"

At last he found it: the message he'd thought out the night before and written very carefully at his shaky desk in Mrs. Rasmussen's first floor room, to keep in his wallet for the next time he saw the girl. Even if she couldn't speak or hear, Lonnie knew the girl could read. He was certain the big uneven writing on the placard belonged to her, and now he checked his message over quickly to make sure everything was there. It was. *If you need help,* Lonnie had printed carefully, *help which won't muck you about, if you want to feel safe, phone Dr. Marigold Samson, at 95214378 or go to 22Royston Avenue, Summer Hill.*

"Got a pen?" he asked Clara.

"Will a pencil do?"

"Sure." Quickly, Lonnie added to his message: *And between September 6 and 8, phone*—" He penciled in Pop's number and then crossed it out, realizing that if she couldn't speak or hear, a telephone would be no use to her. He wrote Pop's name instead and beneath it, *Come to 16 Ridge Road, Katoomba.* Then he folded the paper again and closed the girl's cold fingers over it, tightly.

When they reached Katoomba station, there was someone waiting for them on the platform, someone shortish and stalwart, with the kind of bristly gray crew cut that made you think of soldiers.

Pop.

Lonnie froze. He seized Clara's hand and held it tightly. Behind them, the train waited at the station; there was still time to get back on it and ride on through the hills to Lithgow and then all the way back to town again.

Clara glanced at him. "What's the matter?"

"It's …" he trailed off. A red-faced Pop was striding jauntily toward them.

"Your pop?"

"Yeah."

Clara giggled. Behind them, the train was pulling out— too late to run, too late for anything because Pop was upon them now, the toes of his black shiny shoes almost touching the tips of Lonnie's sneakers. Lonnie flinched. Clara's flowers trembled.

"Thought I'd come up and meet your train," said Pop pleasantly.

Lonnie stared at him, transfixed. Pop hadn't met the train

since Lonnie was twelve, the very first time he'd come up to visit on his own. Close up, he could see that the flaring color of his grandfather's cheeks was embarrassment, not rage. Lonnie stuck out the hand that wasn't holding Clara's. "Great to see you," he mumbled.

"Same here," Pop mumbled back.

Lonnie squeezed Clara's hand. "And this is—"

"Clara," finished Pop, and leaning across the damp bouquet of flowers, he kissed her on the cheek.

40 SERAFINA

Lily had finished her packing, and now she stood outside on the rickety wooden porch gazing up at the sky. This looked like the kind of party weather Nan and her imaginary companion had been hoping for; even in busy Roslyn Avenue, sandwiched as it was between two main roads, the scents of newly mown grass and early roses trembled in the air, and the sky was cloudless except for one tiny white wisp, small as an old lady's handkerchief, that, even as Lily gazed, began to dissolve in the air. And the next day, according to the weather forecast, would be perfect, too.

Good weather brings bad luck, thought Lily gloomily. Hadn't she read that somewhere? And it could quite easily come true: up there in the hills Pop and Lonnie might already have quarreled, and Lonnie and Clara could be on their way home again. Nan might be crying softly or sitting out in the hammock whispering to her imaginary friend; Pop might be storming around the lawn.

"Lily?" Her mother's flushed face—she always got into a tizzy when packing—peered around the edge of the screen door. "Lily, are you all ready?"

Lily nodded.

"Well, would you mind standing out front? I'm expecting Mrs. Nightingale's family any minute now, and I don't want them to miss our house." Marigold tucked a straggling piece of hair behind her ear. "You know how people do."

"Because there's no number on it," Lily informed her.

"What?"

"No number. It fell off the gatepost ages ago."

"Oh, is that why? We'll have to nail it on again."

"You mean I'll have to." Before her mother could reply, Lily wandered off into the street and stood there kicking at the gatepost like a four-year-old.

"Miss? Miss?"

Lily stopped kicking and looked around. A shiny blue car had stopped beside their house. Its window slid down and a worried little mousy face peeped out at her. "Is this Roslyn Road?"

Lily nodded silently.

"I wonder if you could tell me where Dr. Samson lives?"

Lily nodded again. It always surprised her to hear her mum called "Doctor"—how could anyone so vague and disorganized, someone who'd got married because she liked someone's *coat*, actually earn a PhD? And yet, Mum had done so—the world, thought Lily, was a very strange place indeed.

"You can tell me?" The mousy lady frowned at a little piece of paper in her hand. "It says twenty-two here, twenty-two Roslyn Road. Only there doesn't seem to be a twenty-two. We've been up and down four times."

"It's here." Lily gestured vaguely at the house behind her and caught an expression of dismay that flit across Mousy's tiny features as she took in the unkempt hedge of cotoneasters and the sagging gate. "Dr. Samson lives *there*? We thought it was … abandoned."

"It looks better inside," lied Lily. Smiling, she moved closer to the car. "I'm Lily, Dr. Samson's daughter. Mum sent me out to make sure you didn't miss the place."

"Oh!" Mousy's tiny paw went to her mouth. "I'm sorry if I sounded ..."

"That's okay," said Lily brightly. "It does look a bit untidy. We keep it that way to frighten burglars off."

"Oh," said Mousy doubtfully.

"And we're not staying here this weekend anyway. We're all going to Nan and Pop's place in the hills."

Mousy gasped. "You mean, the arrangement's fallen through? You're not taking Mum after all?"

"'Course we're taking her."

A male face loomed darkly over Mousy's shoulder. "If we could just speak to Dr. Samson for a moment ..."

"Stop all this *fussing*!" The rear door of the car snapped open, and a sharp-eyed old lady stepped out onto the pavement.

Lily and Mrs. Nightingale looked each other up and down. Lily saw a tall old lady with white hair woven into a silky coronet of braids—a well-dressed old lady, she noticed with some surprise. Most of Mum's lame ducks dressed oddly, one might almost say fantastically, in styles they'd grown fond of many years, or even decades, earlier. Others wore what Lily called "random" outfits: items picked up from here and there, items that didn't match or sometimes even belong to them. Mrs. Nightingale wasn't a bit like this: she wore a light woolen dress in a deep cool shade of green, with a brown leather belt and brown shoes of the exact same shade. The jacket she carried over her arm was patterned in soft muted checks of fawn and lavender and green.

Mrs. Nightingale saw a stocky girl with wild black curls and fierce black eyes, red cheeks, and something strangely familiar about the jawline and the way she held her head. Mrs.

Nightingale had experienced this same unsettling familiarity with Dr. Samson so that first the good doctor, and now her daughter, reminded Mrs. Nightingale of someone she'd once known and now could not remember.

The driver's door opened and a brown trousered leg emerged.

"Back in the car at once, Phillip!" commanded Mrs. Nightingale. "Didn't you hear me say, 'Don't fuss'?"

The brown trouser leg twitched. "But, Mum, your luggage—"

"Got it!" Mrs. Nightingale pointed triumphantly at the small brown bag she'd placed beside her feet.

Lily picked it up.

Mrs. Nightingale clapped her hands smartly in the direction of the car. "Off you go now, both of you!"

The brown trousered leg disappeared at once, the driver's door closed, and the car slid away smoothly up the street.

"Can't wait to see the back of me," muttered Mrs. Nightingale, sounding rather pleased.

"Are you quite comfortable back there, Mrs. Nightingale?" asked Marigold, slowing for the traffic light at the end of Roslyn Avenue.

"Perfectly comfortable, thank you."

Lily glanced at the rearview mirror and found herself staring straight into their guest's sharp green eyes. "Oh!" she gave a small startled gasp, as Red Riding Hood must have when she caught the wolf in her grandmother's clothing. Not that Mrs. Nightingale looked wolfish exactly—it was just so strange that those green eyes looked so young! *Lame duck* was definitely the wrong term for her.

The light turned green, and they rolled on up the highway, through a shopping district, past the Saturday-deserted grounds of Flinders Secondary. Daniel, thought Lily dreamily and then, sternly, No! Hadn't she vowed to put him out of mind, to devote herself to science, to be strong?

Only she couldn't help herself, couldn't stop from picturing his face: the dark eyes and the long soft lips curving into a smile—and she had to admit that Madame Curie, however admirable, was simply not the stuff from which daydreams were made. Passing the school had made her lapse, she thought, because school was the place where she'd met him—if you could call passing someone in the corridors and on the playground a meeting, or watching his feet from the prompter's box or hearing his voice reciting Shakespeare's lines. School was the only place she'd ever seen him because he lived three whole suburbs up the railway line; she'd looked up his address in the phone book though she'd never actually gone there, never sunk to poor Lara Reid's level and pretended to be jogging past. No, she'd never sunk that low.

Perhaps Daniel didn't live at that address now anyway; it was two whole weeks since he'd been at school …

"In my day," began Mrs. Nightingale suddenly, and Lily jumped, startled, afraid that the old lady had read her mind and was about to say, "In my day, girls didn't have time to spare for daydreams about boys."

"In your day, Mrs. Nightingale?" prompted Marigold.

"There was nothing but crusts and papers." Crusts and papers! Whatever could she mean? Had Mrs. Nightingale been poor in childhood? Had she come from the kind of family that had only crusts to eat and wore newspapers beneath their clothes to keep out the cold?

"And now it's all plastic and chicken bones," said Mrs. Nightingale with a sigh.

Plastic and chicken bones? Did she mean the children of the poor now scavenged chicken bones and wrapped themselves in plastic to keep warm? Both Marigold and Lily felt uncomfortable. Marigold cleared her throat. "Chicken bones?" she echoed.

"On the playgrounds," Mrs. Nightingale explained, a little irritably. "I've been looking at these schools we've passed. I'm talking about playground litter."

Playground litter! Of course! Mrs. Nightingale had once been a teacher. Lily stifled a giggle; her mother dug her sharply in the ribs.

A little farther on, Marigold slowed the car toward the curb.

"What is it?" demanded Lily. "What's wrong?"

"Nothing," replied her mother cheerfully. "I just need to mail these, that's all." She took two letters from the dashboard and handed them to Lily. "Would you mind hopping out, darling, and dropping them in that mailbox across the road?"

Lily snatched the letters and got out of the car.

"Mind the traffic, won't you? Remember to look both ways."

"I'm the sensible one in the family, remember?"

"What?"

"I'm the sensible one in the family! I know my road rules, Mum. I won't get run over."

A small stifled snort came from the back seat. Lily looked through the window and saw Mrs. Nightingale's lips twitch, almost as if she was struggling to suppress a smile. Had

Mrs. Nightingale long, long ago been the sensible one in her family? Clutching the letters, Lily set off across the highway. The city-bound traffic was heavy; standing waiting on the central median, Lily glanced up at the perfect sky that seemed meant for happiness and sighed. She felt bereft, as if she and Daniel Steadman had actually had a real relationship and then broken up—Lily gave a small irritated jerk of her head. Honestly, she was getting as bad as Nan with her imaginary companion.

A gap came in the traffic, too brief for her to cross, though she could see beyond it to the sidewalk on the other side, the houses, the red mailbox, and—and Daniel Steadman stooping to gather up a newspaper from beside his gate. Daniel.

Surely it couldn't be. Surely she was having some kind of hallucination! The gap in the traffic closed, and he vanished from sight. When another gap opened, he'd be gone. Of course he'd be gone.

Only he wasn't. He was still standing in the gateway wearing striped pajamas, tossing the rolled-up newspaper from hand to hand in a gesture that seemed oddly familiar to Lily, as if she'd seen all this before: that house and gate, the mailbox, Daniel in pajamas tossing a rolled-up newspaper from hand to hand. How could she have, though? She'd never been here in her life.

Daniel smiled. At her? Lily didn't know. She ran through the gap in the traffic toward the red mailbox. A car hooted, swerving around her, and she heard her mother's voice call out, "Lily! Be careful!"

"I am being careful," shouted Lily, gaining the sidewalk and thrusting the letters into the box.

When she turned, Daniel was right behind her. His face had

turned a brilliant pink. Because of the pajamas, Lily thought. Because he's wearing pajamas in the afternoon, that's all.

"Hi," she said.

"Hi" was a simple short syllable, but the moment Lily spoke it, Daniel Steadman's eyes widened in surprise. He knew with utter certainty that this was the voice he'd been remembering in his dreams, the beautiful voice to which he'd never been able to put a face or a name or a place except that, mistily, he thought it might have something to do with the Drama Society at school. With the school production.

"It's *you*," he said.

"Me?" Lily sucked in her breath.

Daniel nodded.

"Me?" she said again.

"I kept hearing this voice," he said. "When I was sick."

So he'd been sick—that's why he hadn't been at school. That's why he was wearing pajamas. He was thinner, she could see it …

"I kept dreaming, you know how you do, and there was this beautiful voice—"

"It's not beautiful," protested Lily, laughing, and Daniel insisted that it was.

"Though the funny thing is, I can't remember ever meeting you, talking to you—" He scratched at his lovely feathery hair. "It seemed to have—in the dreams, I mean—something to do with the school production, though I've never seen you at rehearsals."

"That's because I only went one time before you got sick," explained Lily, "and you wouldn't have seen me because I was underneath the stage."

"Underneath the stage?"

"I'm the new prompter. I'm Lily. Lily Samson."

"Oh," he said. "That's it, of course."

She held out her hand to him. He grasped it warmly. They stood there.

"I'm Daniel," he said at last. "Daniel Steadman."

Lily didn't say she knew.

On the other side of the highway, beyond the rush and roar of traffic, a familiar horn blared out. "That's my mum," said Lily. "I've got to go. We're on our way up to the mountains, to my grandpa's place, for his eightieth birthday party." It sounded so normal, thought Lily, exactly as if she had a proper family, one that did the kind of things that other families do—

"Oh," said Daniel. "Well, but—will you be there at rehearsal next week?"

Lily nodded

"So will I!" His eyes searched her face. He seemed to be waiting for her to say something, only Lily couldn't think what.

"Um, so... " she floundered.

"So—so I'll see you there. Next Wednesday?"

"Not much of me," she answered. "Down beneath the stage."

"But after?" said Daniel. "Afterward? We could—" the pink in his cheeks grew brighter, "—we could … go and have coffee somewhere."

"Yes we could," said Lily, smiling.

"Who was that?" asked Marigold, as Lily climbed back into the car.

"No one."

"No one?" Her mother's smile was maddening, but Lily

bore with it, though she felt her cheeks grow hot.

"Just a kid from school, that's all," she said, and from the back seat Mrs. Nightingale murmured, "Ah, young love, true love—" a remark that normally would have infuriated Lily, but that, at this glorious moment of her life, simply made her smile and say with great dignity, "Could be, Mrs. Nightingale."

"You may call me Serafina," said Mrs. Nightingale grandly. "Or for short, Sef."

"*Sef?*"

Lily swung around. Marigold's amazed eyes sought out her passenger's face in the rearview mirror.

"Sef?" they said in strange, shocked unison.

41 ROSE'S JOURNEY

Rose stepped from the train onto the platform at Katoomba. A sloping ramp took her down into the underpass, and then damp steep steps rose up into the street. Long chilly shadows spread across the sidewalk, and she drew her jacket around her; the journey had taken longer than she'd expected, it was getting close to five o'clock, and soon it would be dark. Where should she go now? She was beginning to feel silly, impetuous—perhaps she shouldn't have come? What was she doing? Where was Clara?

"Ask anyone," Jessaline had told her. "Ask anyone, Mrs. Lee. Lonnie told Clara that everyone up there knows Stan."

Right.

A young man in a gray suit was crossing the busy road toward the station, and as he gained the sidewalk, Rose stepped up to him, forcing herself to smile as he glanced at her nervously.

"I'm looking for an elderly man who lives around here," she said. "His name's Stan."

"Stan?"

The moment she'd spoken she knew her question sounded peculiar. Perhaps it was the absence of a second name or the fact that the town looked bigger than she'd bargained for: the road in front of them rushed with traffic, and behind it a long main street of restaurants and craft shops was still busy in this last hour of a Saturday afternoon.

"Stan?" the young man said again, backing away a little, as if, thought Rose indignantly, she'd asked for Lucifer or Mephistopheles.

"Yes, *Stan*," she repeated crossly.

"Sorry, haven't a clue," the young man answered. "I don't live here. Just visiting." And he hurried past her and disappeared down the steps into the station.

"You looking for Stan?"

Rose turned round. She hadn't noticed the tiny newspaper kiosk squeezed in between a travel agent's and a café, or the red-haired woman inside it, her plump, freckled arms resting on the counter. "Think I know who you mean, dear. Red-faced old geezer? Big mouth on him? Bristly gray hair?"

"I'm not sure," said Rose faintly, and yet the description seemed to ring some kind of bell, especially the bristly gray hair. One of those old men in her library who sat reading the newspapers all day? No, it sounded more like that old man she'd met in the park and later on at Strathfield station, the one with the soldier's haircut who'd told her she had a right to see her daughter's room.

"I was only given the first name," she told the freckled lady. "His grandson told my daughter anyone up here would know him—"

The freckled lady smiled. "Sure we know him. Everyone knows Stan. Comes up here to get his newspaper every day."

"Do you know where he lives?"

"Never asked, but it's up that way." She pointed toward the main street. "Round that corner by the post office. Friend of yours, is he?"

"More of ... more my daughter's friend."

"Well, I'm pretty new here myself, love. All the same, I've

noticed him. Noticed him yesterday. Having a party, is he?"

"Um, yes."

The freckled lady chuckled. "Thought so. He had all this party glitter in his beard. You walk on up that way, reckon you'll find someone who knows."

Rose picked up her bag and walked on—up the main street and around the corner to the top of a steep hill. It was almost evening now, and fog billowed up to meet her in gusts of shivery cold air. In those last few minutes, while she'd been talking to the lady in the kiosk, the place seemed to have emptied. Shops were closing, lights coming on, and there was hardly anyone left in the street—no one to ask where Stan lived. And how stupid she must seem, thought Rose, a silly woman bumbling about, asking for a man whose last name she didn't know. She turned a corner and walked on again, the dumb motion of her feet recalling those months after her parents had died, those evenings when she'd walked and walked along the streets of their suburb, walked until she was so tired that when she got home she would sink down onto her bed and fall asleep at once.

She turned into another side street, where the front windows of the cottages were lit and curtains drawn. The long steep street ended in a reserve; beyond it, in the fading light, Rose caught glimpses of mountains, blue and creased, like a big fat quilt, fold on fold on fold. She turned left, then right again, up and down, up—now she was near the station again; she could hear the short urgent hoot of a train. Should she go back home? A seat loomed up suddenly beside her on the nature strip: a bus stop. Rose sat down.

Why had she come here? Because of Clara? Because she was worried about her daughter? She'd worried about Clara being lonely, yet Clara obviously wasn't lonely—she had friends, she was engaged, she was entering another family. Surely it was she herself who felt abandoned, as she'd felt when her parents had died and left her on her own. Her lovely Clara was vanishing, not abruptly, as her mum and dad had, but little piece by little piece. First Clara had left the house, then there had come longer and longer spaces between their coffee meetings, and then—

"Are you all right, dear?"

Rose looked up into a big square smiling face.

"Looking for Stan and May's place, love?"

Rose nodded. She was beyond caring how this stranger knew. "If it's the same Stan."

"Sure it is. Old chap? Turning eighty tomorrow?"

"That's him."

"You're Lonnie's girlfriend's mum, I'll bet. Saw them go past this morning with Stan—she's a lovely-looking girl, your daughter. You must be proud of her."

"I am," said Rose.

"Come up for the party tomorrow, have you?"

"Not exactly. I mean ..." Rose faltered. "I've sort of lost my way."

"They're down there, love." The square-faced lady pointed down the hill. "Second turn on the left. Ridge Road, number twenty-two. Want me to call them for you, tell them you're on your way?"

"Oh! No! I'll be fine. Um, I got lost, that's all."

"Easy to do. It's a funny old place this, if you're not used to it. Small, but you could walk round in circles all day, 'specially when it's dark." She smiled at Rose. "Sure you don't want me to come with you?"

Rose shook her head. "But thank you," she said. "Thank you, Mrs. ...?"

"Lapwing, love. I'm Mrs. Lapwing. Friend of May's from the Gardening Club."

"Thank you, Mrs. Lapwing." Rose picked up her bag. Down the road then, second turn on the left—was that what Mrs. Lapwing had said? Her instructions had been simple enough, yet in five minutes Rose was lost again. She found the first left but not the second. Could she have missed it? It was so hard to tell, with the dark coming on and the wisps of fog sneaking everywhere, her feet hurting and the small bag heavy in her hand. Should she turn back to the station and ask the freckly woman at the kiosk to suggest some small hotel?

Standing there, footsore and undecided, Rose caught sight of a young woman standing beneath the streetlight a little farther down the road. Some kind of New Age girl, she thought as she hurried toward her, noticing the long brown dress and heavy woolen shawl, a New Age girl pointing to the signpost at the corner of the road. Her face looked oddly familiar, as if Rose had seen it quite recently. In the newspaper? Some kind of picture, she thought tiredly, a picture in a book ... of course! Last week she'd catalogued a new biography of the Brontë sisters—this girl looked like Emily Brontë. A gust of fog blew up suddenly and hid the girl from sight. When Rose reached the streetlight, the Emily Brontë girl had gone, and there, in the direction she'd been pointing, Rose saw the sign for Ridge Road. In no time at all she'd found the house, snug in its garden, windows lighted, curtains drawn. She paused at the gate. Clara would be so *angry* when she saw her—Clara would call her a spy.

And then Rose thought of her own parents. She thought of them dying, drowning, the sea surging round them, the broken ferry going down. She knew, now that she was a mother, that they would have thought of her, they'd have worried even as the water filled up their lungs, about what might happen to her in her life. They would have wanted her to be all right, to be happy, to be loved, to be strong and brave.

"Okay, I will be," said Rose. And she straightened her shoulders and walked up the path to the door.

42 CLOUDLESS

Lily couldn't get her head around it all.

First there'd been the meeting with Daniel, so magical and unexpected that had it not been for those small knowing smiles from Mum and Mrs. Nightingale, she might have thought it had been a dream—

And now there was her family. Could this actually be *her* family, all together in one room, with no one quarreling or threatening or criticizing? Pop and Lonnie talking to each other, without a word from Pop about "New Australians," and Clara actually wearing Pop's mum's wedding dress, because, as she told Lily, "Pop wanted me to try it on. He said I looked like it was made for me. Wasn't that sweet of him?"

Sweet? It wasn't a word Lily normally associated with Pop. "He said that? Are you sure it wasn't Nan?"

Clara had laughed. "Of course not."

And Pop was right, thought Lily, because the wedding dress fitted Clara perfectly, the beaded band framing her throat and circling her slight shoulders, the creamy silk flowing like water down her slender body to below her knees.

So Pop wasn't the awful old racist she'd imagined him to be, it seemed.

And Nan wasn't a batty old lady with an imaginary companion because Sef was real. Sef was Serafina. She was old Mrs. Nightingale, who'd been Nan's friend at the children's home almost three quarters of a century ago. It was wonderful but weird all the same, the kind of miracle that happened in fairy tales and certainly never occurred in families like theirs. Strictly unmagical, the Samsons—except this evening, with the light fading over Nan's beautiful garden, and the fairy lights winking in the trees, it was possible to believe they might have their share of magic, too.

Like anyone else, thought Lily sensibly. Why shouldn't we? Just once?

She glanced across the room at Pop. He was standing by the window twitching the curtains aside. She'd noticed him doing this for the last half hour, a puzzled, anxious expression on his face, as if he was expecting another guest to arrive. Now he raised a spotted old hand to his forehead as if his head was aching, and it suddenly struck her that he'd be eighty years old the next day. Eighty! Lily hurried across to him.

"Are you okay, Pop?"

For a moment, it was almost as if he didn't know who she was. Then he recovered. "Right as rain," he answered. "Only ..."

"Only?"

"I can't help thinking there's someone missing from this room, if you know what I mean. Someone who should be here and isn't ..."

Lily looked around. Everyone who should be there was there: Clara and Lonnie talking to Mum, Nan and Sef with their heads bent over Nan's photograph album, herself and Pop—so who could be left out? Who could he mean?

An idea struck her suddenly. It couldn't be. Surely not? Pop couldn't be thinking of—though on such a night even this might just be possible. "You mean my—" Lily struggled to get out the word, "—my dad?"

Pop turned to her with a look of incomprehension.

"I mean," she stumbled, "—Lonnie's dad?"

"Eh?"

"Our, um … father. You know. The one with the coat."

"Him!" Stan roared. "'Course I didn't mean that shifty hippie bugger! What's come over you, girl? You going soft on me, Lil?"

Lily grinned at him. This was more like it. "'Course I'm not." She dug him slyly in the ribs. "But what about you, Pop?" she said, jerking her thumb across the room at Lonnie. "I thought *he* was never going to be your grandson anymore."

"No good keeping up quarrels at my age," said Stan sheepishly. Then his voice sharpened. "Is that—"

"Someone at the door?" finished Lily, who'd heard the knocking too. A knocking so light it was almost furtive, thought Lily, as she followed Pop out into the hall, as if the person on the other side of the door felt they had no right to be there.

Pop swung the door open. A small Chinese lady stood on the doorstep—no, perched on it, thought Lily, perched ready to fly away.

Except when she saw Pop, she smiled, and Pop smiled right back at her. "I've had this feeling all evening someone was missing," he said, holding open the door.

Lily felt her knees go watery as she followed them back into the living room. She'd known it was all too good to be true; of course the Samsons couldn't have a special perfect day like other families. Of course they couldn't! Now Pop had gone and found himself a Chinese girlfriend—oh, poor, poor Nan! Look how she was smiling, chattering away with her old friend. It was obvious she hadn't caught on yet.

Clara had caught on; she was staring at the newcomer, and her face, above the lovely wedding dress, had gone white with shock.

"This is a friend of mine," announced Pop. And then he glanced at his friend enquiringly.

"Rose," said the little Chinese lady. "I'm Rose."

"And I'm Stan," Pop told her.

Lily stared, bewildered, as the two of them shook hands.

Not a girlfriend, then. Otherwise, surely, they'd know each other's names? Wouldn't they? She felt like crying because how could you tell? In their family? How could you ever tell what was going on?

"Mum!" It was Clara. Clara in a blur of creamy silk, flying across the room, Clara flinging her arms around the stranger so fiercely she almost knocked her from her feet.

Okay, Lily got it now. This Rose was Clara's mum. So—so why hadn't she come with Clara and Lon? And how come Clara hadn't known she was coming? Why were they crying? Dysfunctional, for sure, thought Lily with a sigh. They'd acquired a second dysfunctional family. Where was Clara's dad, for a start?

Clara's dad was at Central station. He'd spent the afternoon in his study pacing up and down. Every ten minutes his anxious steps would take him to the window, where he expected to see Rose, returned to her senses, coming back home again, because how could Rose, who had always been rather shy, go off uninvited to intrude upon a houseful of strangers? A house whose location she hadn't seemed quite sure about, except that it was somewhere in Katoomba and its occupant had the first name of Stan?

No, Rose was a sensible woman, Charlie told himself. He knew she was upset. He realized the sudden news of Clara's engagement must have been unsettling, but when she'd had time to think about it, she'd come around to his opinion: that Clara's engagement was no real business of theirs. Rose had gone somewhere to think, he decided—to a park, or the kind of quiet tea shop frequented by ladies of a certain age. She'd calm down, realize he was right, and then come home again.

The afternoon went on and on. Lights came on along the street; ten minutes later it grew dark, and then Charlie knew Rose wasn't coming home. He pictured her walking into Central station, hesitating a moment by the ticket machine, still a little unsure. Then she'd make up her mind: he saw that sudden determined tilt of her chin, the same small movement he'd often seen on Clara. Very carefully, Rose would press the buttons for Katoomba and scoop up her ticket and change. He pictured her entering the train, standing on tiptoe to place her bag in the rack, sitting down on the seat, leaning her head back, closing her eyes. Abruptly, he remembered the fierce look she'd given him when he'd said, "It's no business of ours!"

Charlie left the study and hurried down the hall. He grabbed his coat from its hook by the door and checked the pockets for his keys and wallet. Then he left the house.

At Central he found his hands were trembling; he couldn't press the right buttons on the ticket machine. He went to the window.

"What can I do you for, mate?" asked the man behind the glass.

"Return ticket to Takoomba," said Charlie solemnly. The

worries of the afternoon had caused him to misplace syllables—stress occasionally had this effect on him.

"Takoomba?" the ticket seller queried. "You mean, ah—Toowoomba?"

"No I don't. I mean, I mean Koo-, Koo—"

"Kooweerup? Down in Victoria? Long trip, that, mate, and you'll have to change at Melbourne. Reckon you wouldn't get there till tomorrow afternoon."

Charlie shook his head impatiently. "Not Kooweerup. Kat, Kat—"

"Cattai Creek?"

Charlie knew the man was trying to be helpful, knew he thought this Chinese person might be having trouble with the language. "Be calm," Charlie told himself silently. "Think of something peaceful and perfect and calm." He took a deep breath and slipped into the daydream he often used to send himself to sleep: he pictured his office, neat and orderly, a row of perfect clients waiting on chairs outside his door, truthful, tidy people who had all their details ready and never became angry or confused …

"Are you all right, mate?"

Charlie opened his eyes. "Katoomba," he said quite clearly. "Return to Katoomba."

"Katoomba! Off to the mountains, eh?"

Charlie didn't know what came over him. He told the man proudly, "My daughter has become engaged." He felt his lips stretch into a foolish smile.

"Congratulations!"

"Thank you!"

Charlie found a seat at the back of the carriage, hoping no one would come to sit beside him. Someone did come, right at the very last moment, as the train began to move. A young girl dressed in dusty black—and pregnant, Charlie saw with some alarm. Her pale face was oddly streaked, as if she'd tried to wash it without soap and only made it dirtier. In one hand she carried a battered knapsack, which she placed carefully beside her feet; in the other she held a ticket to Katoomba and the piece of crumpled paper that Lonnie had given to her that morning. The paper was warm from her fingers where, after reading its message and taking in the address, she'd clutched it tightly, all those long, long hours until at last she'd made up her mind.

Her name was Lucy. And as the train sped westward through the dark, she had the unaccustomed feeling that she was going home.

It was almost dawn on the day of Pop's party. Lily had awoken early. Now she sat out on the front steps breathing in the heavy scent of dew-soaked glass and flowers.

They had a bigger family now, she thought. Not only Clara had been added but Clara's mum, and even her dad, who'd arrived the night before on the very last train, bringing with him—of all people—the beggar girl in black whom Pop had been worrying about for weeks. Her name was Lucy, and somehow Lily knew Lucy was with them to stay, and her baby, too, when it came along. There was even talk of Sef moving up into the hills.

And then there was Daniel. He wasn't family of course; he wasn't even her boyfriend, but she was going out with him next Wednesday, after the *Hamlet* rehearsal. The weird fizzy feeling Lily had experienced that time she'd seen him walking down the corridor at school swept over her again, as if some fundamental law of physics had been broached and she and all her thoughts were floating way above the ground. She hadn't been sure she'd liked the feeling then, and she wasn't sure even now. Had Madame Curie ever felt this way? Perhaps she had—because it wasn't simply fizz or air-headedness; it was as if the ordinary world had mysteriously expanded, revealing all kinds of possibilities you'd never known existed or at least not for you.

Lily had thought she was the first one awake this morning and that behind her, in the solid little house, everyone else was sleeping, but now she became aware of a faint sound, like far-off whispered conversation, light steps in the grass. She held her breath and listened. The sound was coming from the very bottom of the garden, from behind the shed, where there was a velvety square of lawn that Nan said had once been a croquet lawn. Lily got up from the step and crept down the narrow path beside the hedge. She peeped around the corner of the shed and saw two old ladies in dressing gowns and slippers dancing slowly around the lawn. It was a sight that would have made Tracy Gilman burst out laughing, and yet Lily thought Nan and Serafina's dancing sort of *fitted*: fitted the beautiful garden and the perfect lovely day she knew was coming, after all. The sky was lightening now. In the distance the mountains were suddenly rimmed with gold, and some-where in Nan's garden the first bird began to sing boldly, high up in the trees.

And from deep inside the house the telephone shrilled. At five on a Sunday morning, who could this be, when all of them—even down to Lucy and Clara's dad—were here?

Lily smiled. She knew who this would be. Not Daniel, Daniel would wait until Wednesday.

Someone who knew to call here at weekends if no one answered back home at Roslyn Avenue, even if Pop bawled him out, called him a shifty hippie bugger or simply hung up the phone.

Someone who lived in Keene, New Hampshire, U.S.A., where, at this very moment, it would still be Saturday afternoon.

Someone who always got her birthday wrong and then remembered six months later.

Someone who'd once called her "Lolly."

Someone who was always promising to visit and, so far, never had …

Back at the house the phone was still ringing as Lily began to sprint across the lawn.

"Answer that phone, someone!" Pop was roaring from his bedroom as she ran into the hall. "Are youse all deaf, or what?"

Lily snatched up the receiver. "Hullo, Dad," she said.